BREAK HER

THE DEVIANT DUET BOOK TWO

RHEA PRYCE

Cover Art: Covers by Marika Veil

Editing: Alexa at The Fiction Fix

Content Warning

This is a forbidden dark romance between STEPSIBLINGS. Please do not turn the page if you are not okay with stepsiblings having a romantic and sexual relationship.

This book contains, but is not limited to, the following content that may be disturbing for some readers: stepsibling relationship, dub-con, mention of self-harm scars, scarification, explicit *kinky* sex scenes, birth control tampering, toxic/possessive/controlling MMC, manipulation, non-consensual bondage, and forced/un-lubed anal play.

Your mental health is so important!

If you have any questions about the content in this book, email me at rheaprycewrites@gmail.com.

Dedication

Rowen isn't finished...

1
Rowen

She. Chose. Me.

And now, I was taking her home.

There wasn't much talking on the two-hour drive, aside from the time we stopped for gas and argued about which chip was superior.

Of course, her favorite had to be the cool ranch tortilla ones. She feigned offense when I called her crazy, though she did try to say my preference for the classic potato chip was boring.

The audacity of this woman.

We both knew I was anything but boring.

I'd have been more than happy to prove it again.

Avery was shaken up at being caught by our parents, but I tried my best to leave the topic alone, at least until we were somewhere she felt safe, somewhere she could break down and let me hold her broken pieces.

I soaked in every moment of the drive. The way she felt behind me, her chest pressed to my back. The way she would squeeze me when we leaned 'too far', which I did on purpose several times, just to feel her tightly against me. The way she got brave an hour and a half in, sticking her hand out so the wind blew through her fingers.

By the time we reached my apartment building, I felt like a desperate teenage boy, unable to think about anything but the fastest way to get into my girl's pants. I needed to get her upstairs quick, before I bent her over my bike and fucked her for the world to see.

The idea of anyone else seeing her perfect, pale curves and hearing her symphony of moans and gasps made me want to punch something. I wasn't about to share Avery with anyone, not if I could help it.

She was all mine.

Mine to love and protect, to break and rebuild. Mine to have and to shield from the world.

"Where are we?" she asked as she removed her helmet. She shook her head, running her fingers through her hair to tame the mess the helmet made of her strands.

"My apartment."

Her eyebrows raised as she looked up at the twenty-story building. "Wow."

"Oh, just wait," I told her, smiling wickedly as I grabbed her hand and led her to the door.

She watched me carefully when we got into the elevator, her eyes narrowing curiously when I held my key card against the sensor and pressed my floor number.

Twenty.

"What's going on?" Her voice was full of confusion.

"What do you mean?"

"Do you really live here?"

"Sure do." I smiled as we approached my floor.

I watched her eyes widen when the elevator doors slid open to the foyer. Her jaw dropped soon after I opened the door to my apartment. She took a few slow steps in before turning to face me in awe.

"This is *yours*?"

I chuckled as I rubbed my chin. "Yes."

"It's...amazing."

"Not bad for a mangy stray, right?" I teased her, and she immediately reddened, wrapping her arms around herself.

"I'm sorry I called you that. I was just..."

"Hey," I said as I walked to her and grabbed her chin, tracing my thumb along her jaw. "Don't go back there. We're here now."

She nodded and bit her lip, her eyes dropping to my mouth. "How about I show you the bedroom?"

She smiled, her cheeks growing even darker as I grabbed hold of her hips and lifted her until her legs were wrapped around me. She was giggling as I walked down the hallway to the primary bedroom.

"This place is *huge*."

"It's the whole floor. Four bedrooms. Five bathrooms. And there's a balcony wrapping around three sides." It was still dark outside, so the city lights shone bright.

"So I'm guessing your apartment wasn't actually being renovated?"

I shrugged as we reached the bedroom door. "I needed an excuse to get closer to you."

She sat up, her lips parted, eyes staring straight into my soul. "That's why you came back? Because of the night at the club?"

"I came back because I realized I was stupid for convincing myself I could be with someone else."

I dropped her onto the bed and crawled over top of her. Her legs instantly wrapped around me, pulling me close.

"You were with someone else?" she asked softly. Her tone was light, but the flicker in her eyes gave her away.

"No one who mattered, Av," I assured her. "I tried to bury you, leave you behind, but it didn't work. No one ever compared to you. And then, that night...when I saw your face, realized what we'd done, it was all over for me." I kissed her lips, quick and sweet. "One taste of you, and I couldn't fathom trying anything else."

She considered my words, letting them sink in, but it wasn't enough. Hurt and jealousy remained. I exhaled slowly, bringing my hands to cradle her back and neck, holding her. She was retreating from me, enough for me to notice, even if she didn't.

"Kitten," I purred, kissing her neck, understanding she needed to know the only woman I worshipped was under me in that moment. "You have all of me, I swear. They were distractions. Bad ones at that."

She didn't answer me, so I flipped us over, her on top of me, and continued as my hands massaged her thighs.

"I was using them to fill the hole inside me. I tried forgetting you, forgetting how badly I wanted you. They weren't enough. Their laughter wasn't like yours. Their eyes didn't sparkle. They were just reminders of how fucked up I was for craving my sister." I pushed my hips up against her, making her gasp. "I didn't want anyone else, Avery. I wanted you, even when you hated me."

"I know it's not fair to be upset. It's just...you were my first, but you'd already..."

"Shh. I understand." I tucked her hair behind her ear. "Trust me, if I hadn't been your first, I might've been tempted to murder the man who was."

She shot me a small, fleeting smile. "Why didn't you say anything before?"

I chuckled. "How do you think that would have gone over? 'Hey, sis, I think you're hot and I can't stop imagining what it would be like to stuff you full of my cock'." She was giggling by the time I finished. "I was a coward, Av. I could have told you—should have—but I was afraid you'd reject me, hate me more than you already did."

"I don't hate you," she said sincerely, leaning down so our chests touched.

"I know, baby." I wrapped a hand in her hair and brought her face to mine. "You're the only thing that's ever felt right, and I don't deserve something so good, but I'll spend every day convincing you I'm worth it."

She didn't say anything, didn't have to. She closed the distance, pressing her mouth to mine.

No hesitation.

Only need.

For me.

2
Avery

I was so close to telling Rowen how I felt, but the words were caught in my throat, like I'd swallowed glass. It hurt, keeping it from him, knowing he wanted to hear it, but I wasn't ready.

Eventually, the thrill of the taboo would wear off.

So, when the fantasy of the stepsister he wasn't supposed to touch faded, leaving just us, would I be enough for him? Could I keep him happy and fulfilled once everything died down and we sank into normalcy? Would he still choose me? Choose us?

I couldn't fathom losing him. Not now, not when I'd already lost so much.

So, the truth dangled on the edge of my tongue, hoping he didn't need to hear those three words yet.

His hands dug into my hips, grinding me on his cock in a steady rhythm. He was so hard, I could feel him through our clothes.

"Stay," he told me after flipping me onto my back.

I watched him carefully as he disappeared through a door—which I assumed was a closet—and reappeared holding bundles of rope and a vibrator.

My heart thumped loudly. My thighs clenched together.

"I'm so glad I was prepared to have you over," he said with a wink, setting down the items on the bed beside me before leaning close. "How does that make you feel, Av? Knowing I'd already decided you would be here, in my apartment, with me?"

I licked my lips. "Makes me wonder why you're so goddamn cocky."

He laughed at my remark, leaning closer until his breath tickled the shell of my ear. "We'll see if that attitude is still here when I have you tied up and helpless, begging for a release I might not grant you."

I shivered, knowing he meant every word of his threat.

He pulled back and grabbed the rope before reaching for my wrists. I didn't resist. I had so much to prove to him, to myself. There was power in giving in to him. Now was my chance to show him I was exactly where I wanted to be—tied up, spread, claimed, and utterly his.

He worked quickly, like a man on a mission, a man who *needed* this. Before I knew it, my hands were tied together, and he was securing the rope to the metal loop in the middle of his headboard.

Fucking psycho.

"What's so funny?" he asked, catching my grin.

"Just can't believe you have a loop on your bed to tie me to."

His grin widened, and it made my stomach fill with butterflies. "I've had lots of time to think of where and how I'd be fucking my sweet little stepsister once I lured her here."

Oh shit.

He reached into his boot and pulled out his knife. His hands were steady as he sliced through my clothes, leaving me in a pile of tattered fabric.

"Rowen!" I laughed.

He wasn't smiling back, though, his attention elsewhere. His fingers grazed my ribs, warm and firm, just below the bandage.

There was only a slight ache left, but now that he was staring at it, it might as well have been on fire. His fingers pulled at the tape until he revealed his initials.

'RBT'

Rowen.

Blake.

Thompson.

The stepbrother I was meant to hate yet found myself madly in love with instead.

"Perfect," he muttered, mostly to himself.

Then, he reached for the vibrator.

I shivered, my body remembering just how well this man wielded this particular weapon, how it nearly took me out the last time.

"I want you begging," he said as the low buzz of the vibrator filled my ears, sending a tremor through me. "I want you begging me to stop. I want you to cry and scream and offer me anything I want to stop torturing your little clit." He pushed the vibrator against my inner thigh, making me jump. "And I want to say no."

I whimpered.

He slid the vibrator between my thighs—not inside me, but just enough to tease. My hips arched instantly, and he smiled victoriously.

"You're already close, aren't you?" He trailed the vibrator up and down my slit, ensuring I was kept on the edge. "You're such a slut for me, Av. Look at you, dripping on your stepbrother's bed."

"Please," I choked out, the feeling of being right on the brink of an orgasm driving me mad with lust. Everything was tight, needing to be released but unable to do so without his permission.

"No one will ever see you like this, broken and desperate. No one will ever make you feel the way I do."

He moved the vibrator, giving me a little more stimulation, making me gasp. My body jerked when he turned it up a level, my wrists yanking at the ropes, thighs shaking.

"Rowen. Please. More." I could barely form thoughts, let alone sentences. It was overwhelming, nearly painful, being so close to the one thing I needed.

He'd reduced me to a mindless sex toy in a matter of minutes.

"Remember this, Av. Remember it was you who asked for more." He kissed my knee, slow and teasing. "And I gave you exactly what you begged for."

He turned the toy up once more—the highest setting—and dragged the toy in harder, deeper circles.

I shattered for him, moaning his name as pleasure took over. My toes curled, my stomach tightened, and then, I felt it. My mouth wouldn't tell him to stop, and my cheeks were already hot with embarrassment.

I felt the warm splashes on my thighs as I screamed, but Rowen didn't let up, didn't pull away. He kept the vibrator on my clit. Even as my body convulsed. Even as I squirted repeatedly with each wave of pleasure.

"Look at that. Soaking the bed for me. Such a good girl for your stepbrother." I felt his lips against my inner thigh. "You didn't hold back, did you? Fuck, Av, you're so wet."

It didn't end after I was done. He didn't even move the toy; he just kept it right in place. I had two seconds to prepare myself for another orgasm.

"There you go," he praised me. "Let me make you feel good. Let everything fall away so you can focus on how amazing it feels to be my little toy."

My toes curled, my head pressed back into the pillow, succumbing to the intense pleasure. Every muscle in my body was tight. Every word I tried to say came out as a moan.

He held steady, no matter how hard I tried to move away from the toy. I held my breath until the pleasure passed, and only then did he pull the vibrator away.

3
Rowen

Avery was still gasping, still shaking when I untied her wrists.

I loved it when she was like this—speechless, lips swollen, cheeks red, thighs still twitching from the orgasms I dragged out of her.

I was about to flip her over, fuck her from behind, when she quietly whispered, "Can I touch you?"

One of my eyebrows raised. "You can always touch me." I grabbed her hands and slid them up under my shirt, letting her touch me, wondering if she could feel the way my heart pounded in my chest just for her. While her hands explored my abs, I pulled my shirt over my head. "You can touch me all you want while I fuck you."

She shook her head. "I want to...try something."

"What's that?" I pressed a kiss to her nose.

Her cheeks flushed pink, and she bit her lip before her eyes trailed down to my...

Oh. OH!

"You want to suck me off?" I asked teasingly.

She smacked my shoulder weakly, her whole face turning red. "Don't say it like that."

"It's so cute when you act all innocent. Kinda fits the image, right? Sweet little stepsister on her knees for her depraved and corrupted stepbrother."

Her breath hitched, and for a split second, I thought I might've taken it too far for her, but then she reached up and grabbed the hem of my jeans, working to unbutton them.

"Fuck, Av. Are you sure?" I asked, getting up and removing my pants and boxers for her.

She nodded and got off the bed to kneel in front of me. Her hands trembled as she reached for my cock, already twitching at the thought of her lips wrapped around it.

Her fingers curled around me, hesitant but warm, and I watched in awe as her lips wrapped around the head. I hissed through my teeth when she descended a few inches.

Her eyes flicked up, wide and nervous.

"You're doing so good," I murmured, brushing her hair back. "Keep doing that."

She kept going, even though it was awkward and messy. It felt so fucking good. She was trying to please me—not because I was forcing her, but because she genuinely wanted to.

I gritted my teeth, watching her cheeks hollow as she sucked a little harder, her eyebrows knitting together in focus.

Her mouth was so warm and wet. I'd fucked it before, but I'd never had it soft and willing like this. It was heavenly, easily the best blowjob I'd ever had, all because it was *her*.

Avery was sexy, by far the most stunning woman in the universe. She could've worn a potato sack and not washed her hair for weeks, and I'd still be hard as a rock just looking at her.

Which was why I was about to come down her throat like a teenage boy, mere minutes into being touched.

"Slow down," I told her when I felt my thighs tighten.

She didn't.

"Avery..." I warned, my voice tightening.

She still didn't stop, so I grabbed her hair and dragged her mouth off me with a pop. My free hand took over, stroking my cock, nearly at the finish line already.

"I don't want my cum disappearing down that pretty little throat when there's such a beautiful canvas to paint with it," I said, looming over her.

"What do you—"

"I'm going to show you who you belong to, Av. Mark you as mine so you don't forget it."

She didn't answer, but she didn't fight me either. My little stepsister sat there, obediently, as I painted her with my cum, groaning while the white strands fell onto her chest. Once I was done, I leaned down, pressing a kiss to her temple.

She started to stand, but I wagged my finger at her. "Not so fast. I'm not finished with you."

She watched me with careful eyes, her chest rising and falling rapidly, her teeth trapping her bottom lip between them. I lowered to my knees in front of her, still towering over her. My fingers pinched her chin, making her look at me so I could lean in and kiss her.

She hissed when I sucked her bottom lip between my teeth and bit down. I didn't stop until the metallic tang of her exploded on my tongue.

"Fuck, Av," I groaned as I leaned back. "Even your goddamn blood tastes like heaven."

She whimpered—music to my ears—and swiped her tongue over her wound.

I ran two fingers across her chest, gathering some cum, and lifted them to her mouth.

"Open," I ordered.

When she did, I ran my fingers over her tongue, spreading my cum, making sure she was coated before shoving them to the back of her throat, gagging her. I pulled back then choked her again, loving the way her hands stayed at her sides and her eyes watered.

Such a good fucking girl—just for me.

I gagged her a third time before letting her close her mouth.

She scrunched up her nose, struggling with the new taste and sensation, but she swallowed my cum down anyway.

Before she could say anything, I stole her mouth again, forcing my tongue inside, tasting her blood and my cum together. She kissed me back, her lips moving with mine, trying to be as forceful as I was, but I dominated the whole thing.

She was panting when I grabbed the hair at the nape of her neck and pulled her back. I made her stay like that, looking up at me, as I spread the mess over her chest, across her nipples, down her stomach.

"Look at you, Avery," I taunted. "Covered in your stepbrother's cum, inside and out, like a dirty whore." I slid my fingers past her lips again. "Suck them clean."

She did, keeping her eyes glued to mine the entire time, her mouth vibrating around my fingers as she moaned.

"Does the sweet little stepsister like the taste of her stepbrother's cum?"

After a moment, she nodded, her lips still wrapped around my fingers.

"There's no more pretending what we have is wrong," I told her and then withdrew my fingers so I could tease her lips with mine. "I'm yours, Av, and it's only a matter of time before you admit you're falling for me too."

She blinked, lips parted like she didn't know what to say.

She didn't need to.

"Let's get you cleaned up, baby," I said as I helped her to her feet. "I'll meet you in the bathroom."

She nodded and moved slowly toward the door.

I took the sheets and cleaned up the mess we'd made as best as I could before putting new sheets on the bed and throwing new blankets on top, ensuring it would be clean and comfy for her after the shower.

When I walked into the bathroom, Avery stood in the middle of it.

"You okay?"

My words seemed to pull her out of a trance, and she blinked when she met my gaze and nodded. "Yeah." She fiddled with her fingers. "I was just waiting for you."

At first, I wasn't sure what to say. Not once had Avery let me shower with her, even though we'd had our parents' house to ourselves. I assumed she needed the space and time to process how she was feeling, to process the twisted fact that she was not only fucking but falling for the last person she should've been with.

"Let's get you in there," I finally said.

After the water warmed, I helped her into the shower.

"Shit!" she exclaimed once she got under the stream. "Why is it so cold?"

I stuck my hand under the water. "It's warm."

"Not warm enough," she remarked.

I couldn't help but laugh as she turned the hot water up until it was so hot, I felt like I was in a sauna. "Damn, baby," I teased. "That water is hotter than Hell."

She laughed and reached for some soap. She froze.

Her soap was in my shower, the sweet vanilla scent that haunted me every day.

I waited, watching as it sank in for her.

"You have my soap already."

"I do."

"Did you know I was coming?"

"Well, I was hoping you'd eventually accompany me here, but to be honest, that's not why I have your soap."

I fought a laugh as she turned and looked at me, one eyebrow raised, her eyes full of confusion.

"I told you I was obsessed with you, Av," I clarified, stepping closer to her, making her look up through her lashes at me. "I love *everything* about you." I leaned down, pressing my forehead to hers. "Even the way you smell drives me goddamn crazy. I couldn't have you here with me, so I needed the next best thing: to surround myself with reminders of you."

"What did the other women think when they spotted the bottle of soap?" she joked. "Did you let them lather themselves up so they'd smell like me?"

I slapped my hands against the wall of the shower, caging her in, our mouths nearly touching, our breaths mingling as the hot water splashed everywhere.

"You're the first woman I've ever brought here, Av," I confessed. "I never brought anyone here, and even if I had, I never would've let them use your soap."

I ran my fingers into her roots and tugged, crashing my mouth to hers, claiming her fully with my kiss, shoving my tongue past her lips. She gasped into my mouth as I pushed her against the cool tile, and it had the exact effect I wanted. She arched her body into mine, pressing her chest against me.

"I love you, Avery," I said once I pulled away, leaving us both panting. "I love you so fucking much, it physically hurts."

She started to open her mouth then closed it, and I would've been lying if I said it didn't kill me that she wouldn't say those words back.

But that was fine.

I'd loved Avery for *years*. I had time to accept that my heart belonged to my stepsister. She still needed to get used to the idea of us.

Patience wasn't something I possessed, but I'd wait a whole fucking lifetime to hear her say those three little words.

So, I'd wait until she was ready to tell me how she felt about me, and I already knew it would be worth every agonizing second.

4
Avery

Rowen was still sleeping when I woke up. He looked peaceful, his eyelids fluttering, lips parted on a soft breath. I wanted to kiss him, but I held myself back, not wanting to wake him yet.

The lights came in through the windows, filling the space with a warm glow that countered the deep blues he'd painted on the walls.

I was almost certain the room had been decorated with hired help. There was no way Rowen picked out the art and decor, but the blue...that was definitely his choice. It reminded me of waking up next to him back home.

My chest flared with pain at the thought of home, of my mom. It felt like forever ago, but it was just the night before. I could still see the look on her face, the way her lips curled with disgust, her eyes lighting up with rage.

I wasn't sure what I'd expected to happen when they found out about us, but I didn't think she'd feel so cold, so done with me, when I left. My heart was broken, thinking she was okay without me, fine with me leaving and never coming back.

"Av..." Rowen's voice dragged as his eyes blinked open. "Whoa," he said when he noticed my tears. He pulled me to his chest. "What's wrong?"

I wiped my wet cheeks. "Nothing. I'm okay. I just...I wasn't expecting her to be *so* angry."

He hugged me tighter, pulling me on top of him. "I'm so sorry, baby. This is all my fault."

I shook my head. "No, it's not. I made my choice." I offered him a smile, and relief flooded me when he smiled too. "And I'm happy with it."

"Promise?" he asked, a slight hint of hesitation in his eyes.

"I promise," I said before kissing him to seal the deal.

His hands cupped my ass, and he moved his hips against me. His cock was already hard, rubbing against my pussy. I found myself moving faster, wanting more.

"If you don't stop, I'll have no choice but to give you another round of last night."

I halted, lying still against him. "So, how did you even afford this place?" I realized how rude I sounded and quickly added, "I'm so sorry. I didn't mean anything by that; I was just curious. You don't have to tell me."

He laughed. "I like that you're curious about me. It's about time the tables turned. I created an app in college for a project. I developed an algorithm that optimized hospital shift allocation based on available staff and patient needs. After schedules were uploaded, along with patient records and their schedules, staff would have an easier time ensuring everyone's needs were met. It wasn't perfect, but I had multiple offers for it by the time I graduated. Sold it for a few million dollars. Turned around and invested that, and I had some really good luck pretty quickly. Now, I analyze and consult other app developers on their projects."

I was shocked at all he'd accomplished already. I sat up and looked him in the eyes. "You've done so much with so little. Do you realize how crazy that is? Do you know you're probably the only one your age who *earned* the penthouse he bought? How are you not being called up for interviews and biographies and shit?"

He beamed as he listened to me. "I did it all under a pseudonym."

"Why would you do that?"

"I guess I didn't want to make a big deal out of it." He rolled over to be on top of me, trying to change the subject by kissing me, but I avoided his attacks.

"Did you ever tell your dad?"

His eyes dimmed. "He didn't give a shit about me after I left."

"Because of me..." My chest was heavy, guilt-ridden.

"No," he spoke, softly but sternly. "It wasn't you, baby. I was an idiot for watching you like that, leaving myself all exposed. I was bound to get caught."

"Do you regret it?" I chewed my bottom lip.

His forest green eyes grew darker. "Not one bit."

***

"Should I call her?" I asked him, staring at my phone like it would give me all the answers.

"And say what?" Rowen said as he ate his breakfast.

"Check on her? I don't know. It's driving me crazy not knowing what's going on over there."

It had been a couple of days since we'd left in the middle of the night on his bike, and I hadn't heard from my mom since. Rowen said his dad hadn't contacted him either, but he also said that wasn't atypical.

There was a mischievous sparkle in his eyes before he mimicked typing on a phone. "'Hey, Mom, I just wanted to see if you were okay after finding my stepbrother balls deep inside me after confessing his undying love. I know it's hard to accept, but I need you to understand—I'm addicted to his cock.'"

"Rowen!" I exclaimed with a laugh.

I took his plate as his punishment, scarfing down a slice of bacon.

"You're going to regret that," he said, narrowing his eyes as he stood from the bar seating and stalked around the island to where I was. "Apologize."

A smile spread on my face before I could stop it. "Awe. Is big brother upset his little sister stole his food?" I snatched another slice, cramming it into my mouth.

His eyes widened as his jaw dropped. "You, woman, are a fucking menace." He was pointing at me, poised to pounce.

"Doesn't feel too good when someone takes your food, does it?"

"Is that what this is about? Revenge?" He huffed a quiet laugh, but the way his eyes darkened was anything but funny. "I'll teach you a thing or two about revenge, little kitty."

The way he said my nickname, low and growly, made my body shiver. He smirked, knowing the effect he had on me.

"You get away from me," I shrieked once he started coming after me. "I never did anything to you for you to avenge!"

I'd nearly made it to his couch in the ridiculously massive living room with huge open windows that showcased the balcony.

"Try years of painful erections I couldn't relieve inside your slick, desperate cunt."

Oh shit.

I liked knowing I'd been driving him crazy too, even if it was in a different way than he did me. I'd had time to think about the things he admitted to doing: the stalking, standing outside my window, sleeping in my bed. At first, I was shocked, violated, knowing he'd taken the liberty to do all of that without my knowledge. The longer I sat with it, though, the hotter I found it.

His deep obsession.

His need to be near me, even if I wasn't physically present.

The fantasy he'd refused to let go, no matter how much time had passed or how mean I was to him.

He even let me look inside a box of my things he'd collected over the years—his trophy case. I shouldn't have been shocked, considering the man had bottles of my soaps in his apartment before I ever set foot inside, because he missed smelling me. The box contained all sorts of things, like old panties, some lipstick, and even a pink baby doll gown I thought I'd lost.

He was expecting me to lose it, probably call him crazy again, but I offered to put it on instead.

We never made it that far, though, because I made the mistake of undressing *in front* of him, and he pounced before I could put the dress on.

"What filthy thoughts are filling that pretty little head, kitten?" he whispered, slowing as he caught up with me in front of the fireplace.

I inched toward the balcony door. "How could you have possibly—"

"It's written all over your face." He was smug, eyeing me like a prize he'd already won. "You're such a slut, I wouldn't be surprised if all you thought about was my cock." His footsteps were slow, measured.

I rolled my eyes at him. "You wish."

"Av..." he said warningly as I reached for the door handle. "Don't you *fucking* dare."

I ignored him, pushing it open and stepping onto the mezzanine.

It was impossible to get far, though, because Rowen closed the distance between us in three seconds. He grabbed my hair and dragged me over to the furniture, quickly pinning me over the back of the nearby couch.

"Have you not learned your lesson?" He leaned down until his lips were brushing my ear, his hips grinding his hard cock against my ass. "Did you really think you could get away from me?" He smacked my ass, and I yelled out. "You will *never* escape me, baby. You let in the goddamn monster, and there's not a damn thing you can do to get rid of him. There's no changing your mind or calling a break. You're mine now, and I will do everything in my power to keep it that way." His voice was thick with need.

I shuddered, goosebumps erupting all over my skin, his words burrowing so deeply, they were ingrained in my bones.

5
Rowen

She was still breathing hard, wiggling her ass against my cock.

I could tell she was trying to bite back her moans, but she was failing to remain quiet.

I made her feel too good. Her body would always recognize mine, respond to me.

"Feel that shiver running through your body?" I asked her as I hiked up the bottom of the shirt she wore—my shirt. "You *love* this. You *wanted* this." She gasped as I slapped her ass again, my handprint popping up immediately. "The whole damn apartment, and you chose the balcony? You knew I'd catch you out here, little kitty. Did you want me to fuck you out here?" Another slap, then another. She whimpered. "Out here, where someone might see you? Get a good look at my slutty little stepsister?"

"No," she murmured half-heartedly.

I shoved her knees apart with my leg and pulled her panties down to her thighs, noticing the way she already trembled in anticipation.

"You're already so fucking wet. Look at this." I slid my fingers between her thighs. "This is what I have to deal with. A bratty little stepsister who runs from me and lies while she drips like a bitch in heat. I've barely touched you, kitten. What were you thinking about?"

"Nothing..."

I shoved two fingers inside her without warning. She choked on a moan, her body fighting mine for a split second before her ass pressed back, giving me more access.

But I withdrew my fingers and slapped her ass instead.

"Tell me the truth, Av," I said after she screamed.

My fingers returned to her cunt, and I curled them, hitting the spot that made her knees buckle. She moaned, just like I knew she would. I felt her pussy clench around me, holding me.

"Last chance." I started to pull my fingers from her again.

"You!" she rushed out. "I was thinking about your little trophy box with all my things in it."

Oh... Oh, Avery.

"Did that turn you on?" I slid a third finger inside her, stretching her wider. "Knowing that even though you hated me, I was obsessed? Stealing your panties and watching you sleep? Even lying in your bed?" She was already panting, so I moved my hand faster. "I've been circling you, baby. From the very beginning. I'm the fucking lion, and you're the innocent lamb."

She turned to look at me, eyes wide, lips parted, cheeks pink. "Rowen," she gasped.

"Tell me you love this. Tell me you need it. Need me."

Her body shook. "I need you."

"That's right." I pulled my fingers out slowly and wiped her arousal on her ass. I kept one hand on her back, holding her steady, reminding her of her place as I undid my belt. She froze when the leather slid free with a pop. "Head up," I commanded.

When her head shot up, I wrapped the belt around her neck, looping the end through the buckle to form a leash. She struggled for breath when I tightened it, but her hands remained on the couch, trusting me, knowing I'd push her but never give her more than she could handle.

I lined my cock up with her entrance and thrusted forward, filling her in one, swift move. She screamed, and my eyes rolled back at the sound.

Avery's cunt was mine to wreck, mine to own.

"You like that?" I snarled, keeping the belt tight against her throat, listening to her gasp for air as her ass wiggled, her entire body begging me to move, to relieve some of the pressure. "Of course you do. You love being used by your stepbrother. You love feeling his huge cock stretch your tight little pussy."

I eased up on the belt so she could breathe but kept it in my hand, a constant threat.

"Please fuck me," she begged.

"I won't stop until you're ruined for everyone else, until you have every fucking vein of my cock memorized."

"I want it," she said desperately, trying her best to move against me, but she was helplessly pinned over the couch.

"That's my girl."

I fucked her hard, unforgiving. Her hips would be bruised from being rammed into the couch. Her pussy would be sore.

But she loved it.

I pulled the belt again, yanking her head back, and slapped her ass. She screamed, and I did it again.

"Scream louder, baby. Make sure the whole damn city knows you're a slut for your me." I released the belt, grabbing her hips instead. "Say it, Av. Yell for me. Say you love your stepbrother's cock."

"I love my stepbrother's cock," she cried out.

I rewarded her with a brutal thrust, using her hips as leverage to fuck her even rougher than before, pounding into her so hard, the couch scraped across the floor.

Her moans echoed off the windows, her pussy spasming around me. She didn't have to tell me she was close. I felt it.

"Are you gonna come for me like a good girl?"

She nodded desperately, moaning with each thrust of my hips, pushing her ass out, chasing her orgasm. Her body stiffened as the climax overtook her.

"Just like that," I praised her, chasing my own pleasure. "Such a good girl, coming on my cock. *Fuck*. You're squeezing me. It feels so fucking good when you do that."

And then, white-hot pleasure exploded in my head, my thighs tightening as I spilled into her. Our pleasure mixed, a hot mess of cum, making her slick.

She was silent, still, when I pulled out. I watched my come spill out of her, dripping down her thighs. Something inside me shifted at the sight, knowing this wouldn't be the last time I filled her up like this.

I needed more.

"You're mine forever, Av," I muttered as I helped her stand, holding her back to my chest, our bodies sticking together.

"Forever," she muttered.

I gathered her into my arms and carried her back inside to fuck her on the bed, to remind her *I* was the one carved into her skin, and she'd never escape that.

6
Avery

"Got it," he said once he closed the door behind him.

He held up the tiny purple box.

Plan B.

Because my stepbrother decided it was a good idea to come inside me on the balcony the day before, not knowing if I was on birth control.

I wasn't.

Rowen followed me to the kitchen, where my glass of water awaited. It had already been nearly twenty-four hours since he came inside me, thanks to being brought back inside and fucked all day by the damn sex addict. What he'd done didn't register in my sex-melted brain until nearly midnight, and Rowen assured me he'd grab some in the morning.

He also admitted to coming inside me at least three more times.

A baby was the last thing we needed.

Stepsiblings raising a kid together? We needed to sort out our own shit before ever considering bringing life into a world more fucked up than we were.

"Thank you."

He peeled the box open and extended his hand, the small white pill in his palm.

I stared at it for a moment then swallowed it.

"Good girl," Rowen murmured as he came closer, a fresh cup of coffee in his hand.

I felt relieved, like I could breathe knowing it was taken care of.

He took a sip of his hot drink then lifted me onto the counter. The cold surface was like needles on the backs of my thighs.

"Feel better?" He tucked a strand of hair behind my ear, and my entire body reacted, already begging for more of his touch.

"I do. I'm just sore now."

He smiled, the sadistic part of his soul loving that I was aching because of him. "I'd be more surprised if you said you were totally fine." He kissed the side of my head. "That you didn't feel me with every step you take."

I shifted my position, pushing him away.

"Hey," he said, leaning back to look me in the eyes. "Everything okay?"

"We need to talk about yesterday." My voice came out small, like I wasn't sure of myself. I hated it, the way he made me question everything. "You should've pulled out. You *always* pull out."

He looked away, his jaw ticking before he pinned me with a dark gaze. "I couldn't help it, Av," he murmured as he ran his hands down my arms, slow, deliberate, like he was trying to memorize the way I felt. "You felt so good. It was sexy knowing you were full of me all night, even when I wasn't inside you."

"I'm not on birth control, Rowen."

He didn't look surprised or worried. He just smirked, and his arms snaked around me, pulling me close. The heat of his body seeped through our clothes, burning my skin, nearly making me forget why I was so upset to begin with. He grabbed my chin, lifting until I was looking up at him, his eyes darker than ever.

"I'll take care of that," was all he said before planting a firm kiss on my lips.

"What does that mean?" I said, my voice back to being small, wishing he'd kiss me again but knowing I had to stand my ground, get answers.

His grip remained on my chin. "I'll handle everything. You'll have your birth control on the doorstep by tomorrow morning."

"I just don't want to get pregnant," I whispered.

"You won't," he said just as quietly. "Not until I say so."

My breath hitched, and I tried to pull away from him, but he held me steady, forcing me to maintain eye contact. His warm eyes and soft smile didn't match what he'd just said, what he'd just insinuated. His love, his obsession, felt heavy, but I knew he didn't mean anything malicious. Rowen just wanted to be loved back, as deeply and madly as he loved.

The hand on my chin moved to my inner thigh, rubbing a spot that made my thoughts freeze up and my brain stop working.

"You look tired." He chuckled.

"I didn't sleep much."

His lips were nearly touching mine, so close, I could taste his breath. "That's my fault, isn't it?"

The way he said it made my cheeks burn. "Might need different bedrooms if you keep this up," I joked, but the air shifted.

His eyes changed from dark and dominant to wild and worried. He wrapped both arms around me again, pulling me as close as he possibly could without me crawling inside him, holding me like he didn't want to let go—couldn't.

"Are you okay?" I asked, melting into his warmth, reassuring him I was there.

"I'm perfect. I've got you." He kissed the top of my head, tender, lingering.

Was he even aware of the tremor in his arms? The tightness in his voice?

He was scared, but of what?

I wasn't sure I wanted to ask, not sure I could handle peeling more layers of Rowen back just yet, knowing there was more he'd yet to show me, knowing he was holding himself back for my sake, to protect me, to keep me from leaving.

Was that what he feared?

Because it felt as though he was holding me like he was already losing me.

***

"Rowen, *please*," I begged as he grabbed his laptop and shoved it into the bag. "I haven't left since we got here. *Ten days ago*."

He'd been working from home the entire time. When I mentioned groceries, a horde of bags arrived. Any time I mentioned going out for lunch or dinner, take-out would show up at the door. He even had a fancy espresso machine delivered when I groaned about wanting a fancy coffee.

I felt isolated.

Since he lived on the top floor, we didn't see neighbors. All the delivery people were gone by the time Rowen made it to the door, insisting he be the one to answer it. Even the cleaning lady who'd come twice since I'd been here must've been invisible, because I'd yet to see her.

My only solace that other people still existed—other than scrolling through social media and seeing everyone living it up for summer—was sitting on the balcony, watching the cars and people pass by every day. Out there, the constant hum of traffic kept me company.

His eyes met mine, and I knew I was fighting a losing battle.

"I don't want you wandering the city without me. You have no idea who's out there, walking the streets, looking for women to turn into the next Dateline episode," he said softly, but there was restraint in his tone. "And you can't come to work with me." He pulled me into his embrace. I didn't even bother uncrossing my arms.

"I feel like a prisoner up here," I admitted. "I don't talk to anyone except you. I still don't even have clothes. I've been wearing yours."

Rowen offered to take me back to the house for my things, but I was too terrified I'd run into either of our parents. I wasn't sure I was ready to face them. Plus, the twenty-three text messages sitting on read that I'd sent to my mother were a clear indication of how she was feeling about everything.

He grabbed my hands. "You look cute wearing my...." He trailed off, noticing my lack of amusement. "Got it." He reached into his pocket, pulling out his wallet. "Go online. Buy whatever you want. Whatever makes you happy."

He handed me a credit card.

"Freedom?" I muttered bitterly. I wiggled out of his grasp and shook one of his arms, as though I could shake some sense into him. "Come on. Don't you want to show me off?" I bit my lip and tilted my chin down to look up through my lashes. "I want to be seen with you. I want to be somewhere loud and crowded and then come back here and complain about it while you remind me why I like staying in."

For the first time, he actually hesitated, and hope filled my chest.

His eyes softened as he sighed, interrupting the silence, though they didn't lose the possessive shadow that was a permanent fixture in them. "I'll be home at six thirty." He pulled me close, his hands behind my head and around my waist. "We'll leave at seven."

I was elated to the point of dizziness, and suddenly, I wanted to jump his bones, even though we'd already had sex twice before he had to get ready for his day full of meetings.

"I do want to show you off, Av. We can go to my favorite club. I'll bring home a dress for you to wear."

"Thank you." I wrapped my arms around him, relieved I'd finally convinced him to let me out. "I'm so excited. Can you send me the name of the place so I can look at their menu before we go?"

"Of course." He brushed my cheek with the back of his finger before cradling the side of my head. "I love you, Avery. Text me if you need anything."

"Yes," I promised him, leaving those three little words out yet again.

He kissed me, unbothered by my lack of reciprocity. It was hard, claiming. It was the type of kiss that made my lips tingle when he pulled away.

After he left, I stood in the silence for a moment, trying to shake the feeling of being locked in a cell when the door clicked shut. Then, I walked through his—no, *our* apartment.

The thought of things being 'ours' made me smile, and warmth curled in my belly.

I wasn't his prisoner, but I understood where he was coming from. Rowen's love for me started years ago. It had time to burrow deep, consume him. It was intense, but it was unconditional.

Some might call it obsessive, but he just loved me. Hard.

At least that's what I told myself as I curled up on the couch and turned the TV on. I grabbed the blanket that smelled like us, like him, and lied against a pillow, my mind spinning.

So what if I didn't leave the house? Why would I, when Rowen had everything I needed? Food, a warm bed, birth control. He made sure I was safe and taken care of. He didn't threaten or hurt me, at least not in a way I didn't like.

He held me tight, washed my body in the shower, always assuring me everything was okay. He told me he loved me, told me I was his.

It wasn't control. I could leave at any time now that he was gone. It wasn't like he locked the doors from the outside or chained me up. All I had to do was turn the knob and step out, use the elevator, and *bam*, I'd be out.

But I didn't.

He just wanted me safe, didn't want to lose me when our story had just begun. It was his way of showing he cared. It wasn't like he had the best role models. He was trying his best.

After the movie, which only captured half my attention, ended, I went to his closet and looked through his clothes, trying to decide what I wanted him to wear to the club. When I hung his outfit up in the bathroom, I caught sight of my reflection.

Pale. Wide-eyed. Happy.

His.

7
Rowen

I was vibrating by the time I wrapped up the final meeting, my hands flexing on the ride home, palms sweaty.

Avery was probably getting ready for the night out, excited to stretch her legs and be around other people, but what I wanted more than anything was to tie her to my bed and edge her until she promised to never leave.

Then, I'd fuck her until she was begging me to stop, until our bed was soaked with her tears...and her juices.

My eyes strayed to the garment bag hanging next to me.

"Big date?" the driver from the chauffeur service, Bernard, asked, smiling at me from the rearview mirror.

He'd driven me many times over the last couple of years, enough to be well acquainted. Bernard was a kind older fellow who valued family and always asked about mine.

"Something like that," I mumbled, wishing he would drive faster, get me to Avery as soon as possible. "I need someone back here at seven."

He nodded. "If I may say so, Mr. Thompson, you look happy." He paused as he turned onto another street. "I've never seen you so anxious to get home. She must be special."

"She sure fucking is."

I knew he was being nice, making small talk, but every second I wasn't with Avery was a second too long. I felt like a shaken soda bottle, ready to explode.

Thankfully, he read me well and left me alone for the rest of the drive, dropping me off at the front door and promising someone from the company would be back at seven to pick us up.

The ride up to my apartment was excruciatingly slow, as was the speed at which the doors opened. I nearly peeled them open myself.

Silence met me when I stepped inside the apartment, my little kitten nowhere to be seen.

"Avery?" I called out.

Nothing.

I took my coat off and set my laptop bag down before walking toward the hall, the garment bag still in my hand. My pace quickened when I heard music coming from our bedroom.

"Avery?" I said again at the doorway.

The primary bathroom light was bright in the dark room. I moved carefully, even though there was no way my steps could rival the volume of the song playing.

When I reached the bathroom, I was met with swaying hips, loud singing, and a hairbrush microphone. She was so adorable, performing a secret concert as she slid across the tile floor.

The song was unknown to me, but I sidestepped into her space after hanging the garment bag on a hook on the door, catching her off guard. Her lips parted, cheeks reddening, but I grabbed the brush from her hand and tried my best to sing along with the lyrics.

I was two or three beats behind and way off pitch, but the sparkle in her eyes and the smile on her face were worth the humiliation. She giggled and shook her head as I spun her around, and then I pulled her body to mine and swayed to the beat.

"You have the most breathtaking smile, baby," I said after putting the hairbrush down. "You're so fucking perfect."

"I wasn't expecting you home for another thirty minutes." Her breathing was unsteady as she leaned up to kiss my cheek. "Did you have a good day?"

"A good day isn't possible without you in it." I grabbed her face with both hands and chased her lips with mine. "But you know...I can think of a way to improve things before we leave for the night."

"Rowen Blake Thompson..." she scolded. "I have to get ready for our date."

She tried to wriggle out of my grasp, but I wouldn't let her go. "Sure I can't change your mind? I can fill your night with orgasms, chocolate, movies, anything you want. We can stay naked at home."

One of her eyebrows raised, and she pursed her lips. "Oh no, mister. You can't trick me with orgasms and food. I won't be so easily swayed." She giggled and pulled away to stand in front of the mirror. "I need to finish getting ready." Her eyes found mine in the reflection. "You have to go. I want it to be a surprise."

I let her push me out of the bathroom, chuckling as she closed the door behind me. As much as I wanted to have her here, the idea of her getting ready just for me, excited to show me, made my heart skip a beat.

While I was tempted to sit outside the bathroom door and listen to her get ready, I busied myself with work emails and tasks from the bed—just far enough to give her space but not enough to drive me crazy.

It was a tempting idea to find some sort of tether to tie her to me tonight, like the ones parents bought for their runaway toddlers. Avery would've been pissed if I presented that idea to her, but it would have been nice for me to know she wouldn't be able to go anywhere, that no one would have a chance to take her from me.

But I'd already made her feel trapped, like a prisoner. She deserved to be happy, and if going out made her happy, I'd take her.

If anyone hits on her, I'll fucking kill them.

It was a quarter to seven when the music turned off. I held my breath as the door swung open, and the sight of her knocked the air from my lungs.

The heels made her perfect legs look longer, drawing attention to them. The dress I'd picked out for her hugged the curves of her waist then flared into a short skirt, only adding more reasons to stare at her legs.

I made a massive mistake with the dress.

The straps were thin, the neckline covering her just enough to make her seem innocent. It was simple, but it was a goddamn trap. She was pure temptation, and I knew when we walked into the club, men would be staring.

She's with you, moron. Forget the lingering eyes.

Half her curled hair was pinned up, leaving the rest falling over her shoulders. Her makeup was natural, save for the way she'd lined her eyes, making them pop.

"You're too beautiful to go out," I complained, but I couldn't fight the smile that took over. "Come here."

She obeyed instantly, coming to stand between my legs at the end of the bed. My hands trailed up her thighs, under her dress, and I grabbed the sides of her panties. When I started to drag them down, she grabbed my wrists.

"Rowen..." She eyed me warily.

"I want to know you're totally bare under there. That at any time, I can reach between your thighs and touch your desperate little cunt." I held eye contact until she dropped her hands. "Good girl, Av," I praised. "Bend over the bed. I decided I want my cum dripping from you tonight."

"Row—"

"Or I could just tie you to the bed and keep you here," I threatened.

I wouldn't have done it.

Or maybe I would have.

I wasn't always sure what I was capable of when it came to Avery, how far I was willing to go to make sure she stayed mine.

She listened, bending over the side of the bed next to me. The way she pushed her ass out, inviting me, made it clear my plan didn't bother her that much.

"Rowen, it's almost sev—"

I slapped her ass, making her yelp. "I don't need long, baby. This isn't for you anyway; it's for me. If you can behave when we're out tonight, I'll give you your reward when we get home."

My cock was out in seconds. I lined myself up with her pussy and pushed forward, filling her slowly without a single break. She moaned, her body softening under my control as the top half of her body sagged onto the bed.

I dug my fingers into the soft flesh of her hips, her pained whimpers making my cock pulse, and started fucking her like a wild man. I wasn't kidding when I said it wasn't for her. While I wanted her to feel good, I preferred if she didn't come before I filled her up. I wanted her right on the fucking edge tonight.

Every step.

Every touch.

Every heated glance.

By the time we got home tonight, she'd be strung-out and desperate for me.

Her cunt was squeezing me as I thrusted into her again and again, railing her as hard as I possibly could.

My thighs tensed as my pace changed, much to her dismay. A deep, throaty grunt rumbled in my chest as my cock twitched inside of her, just before my cum shot out, filling her up. The quick, brutal fuck left a tingling sensation at the bottom of my spine, like I wasn't done.

And I wasn't.

But we had somewhere to be.

8
Avery

"Stay," he commanded as he got out of the car.

"Sir—" the chauffeur started, his door also open, but even he knew it was hopeless to argue with Rowen when he had his mind set on something. So, he shut his door and sighed, giving me a playful wink in the rearview mirror.

I sat impatiently as he rounded the car and opened my door. His hand stretched out, demanding mine, and he helped me to the sidewalk.

"Thanks, Bernard," Rowen said before shutting the door.

His hand settled on my lower back as he guided me toward the club, where a huge line of people stood along the building, waiting to get in. We didn't go to the end of the line. Rowen led us to the front, where a large, muscular bouncer stood, looking terrifying.

"Hey," he greeted my stepbrother with a smile. "Head on inside."

"Thanks, Mike," Rowen replied.

I didn't have time to express my gratitude, since Rowen whisked me inside so quickly, a blast of cool air blew my hair off my shoulders. His touch disappeared as he shook the hand of someone just inside.

"Wow," I whispered, my breath caught in my throat.

My chest was flooded with the beat of the deep bass. The lighting was low, but deep reds and soft whites washed over the room in waves.

There was a giant crystal chandelier above the central floor—a sunken dance floor. Every time the lights hit it, glittering stars painted the ceiling.

Booths made of dark wood and lined with leather bordered the outer edge. They all had high backs, keeping their occupants private.

A second floor, lined with a glass railing, revealed more space, though it seemed like a different atmosphere up there—elevated, more exclusive.

People wearing silk dresses and fancy suits filled the large room, gliding through the space with a sense of ease, as if they belonged.

Just under the music, there was the hum of talking and laughter as they clinked their glasses.

The room even *smelled* expensive, like pricey perfume and exotic flowers.

I tugged at my dress.

What am I even doing here?

His firm, comforting hand found the small of my back just in time to stop me from running out.

He leaned in, his breath tickling my ear. "Breathe."

One word, but it was all I needed to quiet my nerves.

He pulled me to his side, his body heat relaxing mine. Then, we were moving, and while I looked around nervously, feeling like everyone's eyes were on me, judging me, he walked like he owned the damn place. People moved out of his way, watching as we passed, like they were mesmerized by him.

And I understood the feeling.

Rowen led me past a bar, where several people were watching the bartender make their drinks, and into a short hall that led to a staircase.

We were going up?

I followed, ascending the steps until we reached the second floor, where only a few people mingled, gazing out at the groups below. There were several rooms with dark red curtains covering them. Rowen pulled one open and ushered me inside.

It was a private booth with low lighting and a small, lowered table in the middle.

A server wearing all black appeared soon after we sat on the curved bench, my stepbrother's arm settling around me, music filling the silence just enough to make the space more intimate.

"Welcome back, Mr. Thompson," he greeted. "Your usual?"

Rowen shook his head. "We'll take a bottle of something expensive, Kevin. Light and fruity. I want to spoil my date."

I couldn't help but stare at him, looking ridiculously hot, oozing confidence, like he knew people held their breaths around him, that he left them in awe.

As close to seven as we were, it had only taken him a few minutes to get ready.

But it had been more than enough.

He hadn't shaved his five o'clock shadow or styled his hair, but the 'I don't give a fuck' effort was perfect for him.

He didn't own a single suit, so I'd picked out a pair of dark washed jeans that hugged his thighs, a dark gray dress shirt that stretched a little over his broad chest, and his damn leather jacket.

That jacket.

He didn't just look good. He looked delicious, dangerous even, and every woman in the room would notice.

It made me want to cling to him, but we were alone here, and I was afraid he wouldn't understand the fear of losing him to someone better than me, more fitting for him.

"Right away," Kevin said before slipping out.

Rowen turned, catching me staring at him. My lungs suddenly forgot how to work, but I held his eye contact. My heart was thumping so loudly, I was surprised he couldn't hear it. I wanted to kiss him, show him just how badly I wanted him.

His mouth lifted in a small smirk, as though he could hear my thoughts.

"You've been quiet." He brushed some hair behind my ear, making me shiver.

"Just thinking," I responded quietly, my eyes dropping to see his tongue flirt with his bottom lip.

He shifted closer, and his hand landed on my thigh, lighting my nerves on fire. His fingers crawled their way under my dress, getting close but never touching where I wanted him most.

"Thinking about what?" he asked curiously, observing my every movement with intent.

I swallowed. "You."

His fingers grazed over my bare pussy, and I gasped. That was when he dove for my mouth, his tongue leading the charge, filling my mouth, reminding me how he made sin taste like a fucking dessert bar.

I thought he was going to push for more, maybe finger bang me in the booth, but we were interrupted by a throat clearing. Kevin stood between the drapes, eyes down, holding an ice bucket and two glasses.

"Shall I pour your drinks?" he asked Rowen.

My stepbrother didn't even look in his direction as he said, "That would be great."

We were millimeters away from each other, his hand between my thighs, thumb tracing my skin, our breaths mingling, eyes locked.

"So, what are you thinking?" Rowen asked when the server left.

"That you look hot," I admitted, watching his face darken at my boldness. "And it's driving me crazy to be out here. I want to go home," I kept going. "We can go out tomorrow night."

He chuckled, his eyes mocking me. Then, his hand was grabbing my chin, forcing me to look toward the curtains so he could pepper my jaw with soft, punishing kisses. "You did this to yourself, kitten," he growled low in my ear. "You begged for this, dressed me up, and now you want me to take you back home already?" He tugged my earlobe between his teeth, biting hard enough to make me hiss. "We will stay here until I decide I'm ready to go home and fuck your tight, needy pussy until you pass out."

His hand returned to my thigh as the one over my shoulder gripped the hair at the nape of my neck. He angled my head to give him access to my throat, sucking hard enough to leave a mark while his fingers dug into the soft skin of my thighs.

"Rowen," I moaned, my hips moving against nothing.

When he pulled away, he was smiling, like he'd won a game I wasn't aware we were playing.

And that was fine with me, because I wasn't even thinking about the people just outside our booth, dancing to the music under the lights.

I was too focused on him.

9
Rowen

She had no idea how fucking beautiful she looked.

Or the way the lights peeked through the drapes, highlighting her curves, flirting with her plump, red lips. It made my cock harder than it had ever been.

My plan was to get her so worked up, she'd beg to go home. The problem was she begged too early, gave in without much of a fight, when I'd barely even begun torturing her.

I wasn't ready to stop.

But the flush on her cheeks.

The way her eyes were wide and watching, waiting for me.

The goddamn dress *I'd* picked out for her.

Why did I even agree to put myself through this in the first place?

I'd fallen into her trap of thinking I needed to show her off, let her shine bright while making every other man in the room jealous of what I had, but when everyone's eyes followed her as we walked to the VIP stairway, I realized it was more than I could take. I wanted to punch every man who dared to look twice.

Avery was *mine*.

And I had every intention of making that clear to everyone, including my little stepsister.

She was my obsession, and I wanted to remind her of that, show her a devotion so fierce, it left no space for anything else.

"Let's step outside," I said as I pulled away from her to stand.

I could see the need in her eyes, begging me to lay her on the soft cushions and fuck her to the beat of the music.

Not yet, little kitty.

She'd have to earn the right to come on my cock tonight.

Avery was hesitant, but she still took my hand and followed me out of the booth to the railing outside.

"Hands here," I commanded, placing her hands on the metal bar. I grabbed her hips, pulling her back as I used my foot to kick hers apart.

"Rowen..." she said shyly, looking over her shoulder.

"There's no one out here right now," I assured her, and she looked around to see I was right.

I leaned over her, my chest pressed against her back, my hands on the outside of hers.

"No one can see you up here." I pushed my hard cock against her ass. "I could fuck you right here, right now, and as long as you stayed quiet and didn't do that cute little scrunch you do when you come, no one would know." I licked the sensitive spot behind her ear, listening to her breath hitch. "Does that excite my little sister?"

She didn't answer, so I slid my hand up her thigh, under her dress, until I snaked around her waist to cup her pussy. I wasn't surprised to find her dripping.

"Avery Rose..." I said, a slight chastising edge to my voice. "Why are you so wet?"

"Rowen, please," she whimpered as she pushed her ass against me. "I need you."

"I'm not ready."

She sighed dramatically, but I dipped my middle finger inside her, hushing her. When I found her clit, her legs trembled. One of her ankles bent, nearly sending her tumbling, but I grabbed hold of her waist, keeping her upright while I buried my fingers in her wet cunt.

"Do you think any of those people down there know you're up here being fingered by your stepbrother?" I taunted. "What would they say if they figured out how much of a slut you are?"

She didn't want to like it, but her moans gave her away.

"Rowen," I heard from my left.

I turned to see my personal assistant, James, walking toward us. Avery froze, aware of our new company, but I didn't stop playing with her pussy as I stared down the man trying to interrupt us.

She made a pathetic sound somewhere between a whimper and a sigh, like she was ashamed of just how much she was enjoying it.

"James," I said as he got closer.

Avery was covered, but there was no doubt James would know exactly what was going on.

"Didn't expect to see you two out."

I tightened my arm around her waist. "I can't say no to my girlfriend, and she was getting restless in the apartment." My lips curled with a smirk when she stifled a moan. "But we are trying to have a nice, quiet date night if you don't mind."

James didn't budge. "There's something I needed to discuss with you."

"Make it quick," I said as I slid two fingers inside Avery's cunt.

"I think we should discuss it alone." His eyes briefly trailed to my stepsister.

Right.

I withdrew my fingers and pulled Avery to stand. Her eyes barely met mine, and I don't think I'd ever seen her face so red, but the spark of desire remained.

"Go grab a drink from the bar," I told her, soft but firm.

"But the serv—"

"Avery," I said sternly.

She looked confused, irritated we'd been interrupted, but after a second, she turned and walked past James. I turned to look at the floor below, and moments later, she emerged from the shadows, beelining for the bar.

"Make it quick, James."

"I have what you asked for." He reached into his suit and pulled out a small package. "I figured since it wasn't obtained the typical way, you wanted to keep it a secret."

"Don't judge me, James," I warned as I took the package and tucked it into my jacket.

He raised his hands in surrender. "Never." He looked down at the crowd. "You'd better get your girl back up here."

I looked down to see two men approaching her from opposite sides. The bigger one reached her first and started talking to her, so the smaller guy stayed close and watched the exchange. She smiled politely at the first man and shook her head, but he moved closer, invading her space. He took her hand and planted a kiss on the back. She was clearly nervous, but not the good kind, and yet, she laughed anyway.

My blood boiled, and my knuckles turned white as I gripped the railing, wondering if she was enjoying another man flirting with her, if she knew I was watching. She should've been pushing that man away, slapping him across the face, anything to get him to stop, before walking her little ass up here so I could fuck it before we left.

Taking Avery out had been a mistake.

"James," I called out. "I need something else. I'll text you."

He nodded, and I didn't watch him leave as I looked back at my stepsister.

The second man was getting closer, picking up on the first guy's failed attempt.

Why was she just standing there?

Did she like other men flirting with her? Was she enjoying the attention? Was it better than mine?

I growled and pushed off the railing, heading straight for the stairs.

Fuck this.

10
Avery

I didn't need to look up to know Rowen was watching me. I could feel his gaze burning holes into my back.

Good.

I couldn't believe Rowen had continued to finger me when the guy walked up, as though it didn't matter that we were being watched, just to send me away so he could have a secret conversation. My entire body was flaming with blush when I walked, eyes down, past James.

"Drink?" the bartender asked.

"Something strong that tastes good," I said loudly over the music. "I want to get drunk fast as payback to my date."

The bartender nodded, like he knew exactly what to get me. "You got it."

I turned to my right to see a large man approaching. He was average-looking, tall, and muscular. Nothing extraordinary. Nothing like the man waiting for me upstairs.

"Hey," he said as he leaned against the bar.

"Hi."

I could see the bartender preparing my drink, whatever it was, and I bounced impatiently.

"I'm Aaron."

"Avery."

"That's such a pretty name," he replied as he grabbed my hand and placed a kiss on it.

I shouldn't have let him, but I couldn't help the smug satisfaction knowing Rowen had definitely seen that interaction and would lose his shit.

Serves him right for making me leave after getting me so close in front of a damn stranger.

Aaron motioned over another bartender. "Whiskey. Neat." Aaron looked at me. "Can I get you something?"

I shook my head. "I already have something being made, but thank you."

"Are you here alone?"

I looked at the guy attempting to flirt with me, deciding it was best to end this before it got too far. "No. I'm not."

"Here you go." The bartender who'd taken my order placed a pink shot in front of me.

I didn't hesitate to throw it back, but I was shocked to find it was pleasantly tart and sweet, with hardly any hint of alcohol.

"Can I have one more?" I asked him, giggling.

"Sure thing."

I stood there in silence for a while, listening to the song, letting the music wash over me, drowning out my thoughts for a few minutes.

Aaron—who I'd honestly forgotten was still there—cleared his throat, wanting my attention back. "Do you want to dance?" He motioned to my body swaying to the music.

I shook my head. "My boyfriend wouldn't like that very much."

The term 'boyfriend' felt weird slipping off my tongue, but it ignited something deep in my belly that warmed my entire body. I liked the idea of calling Rowen *mine*.

"Here you go." My drink appeared.

I tossed back the shot quickly and decided it was time to find my way back to my *boyfriend*.

"So where's the lucky guy stupid enough to let such a gorgeous woman walk around by herself?" Aaron grabbed my arm gently—nothing threatening, but just enough to make sure I was still aware of his interest.

"Look, I—"

"He's watching her carefully for fuckfaces like you."

His voice sent shivers down my spine. I was so needy for him, so desperate for his touch, I would've stripped naked right there in front of everyone had he asked.

Rowen's arms wrapped around me, pulling me close.

"Hey, you." I looked up at him, biting my bottom lip. "Decided to join the party?"

There was nothing soft or sweet about the way he looked down at me. His eyes weren't playful; they were *feral*, so intense, they pinned me in place.

He was holding himself back, barely restrained. I could tell he needed to rip me apart and take what belonged to him just as badly as I wanted him to.

I raised a daring eyebrow, and, judging by how his jaw ticked, he took the hint.

"Let's go," he demanded, pulling me toward the doors.

"Hang on." Aaron grabbed my arm, playing tug-of-war with Rowen. "She didn't say she was ready to go, man. Have some respect for the lady."

I giggled, but it wasn't because I found anything funny. It was more of a maniacal laugh, knowing Aaron had picked the wrong girl.

Rowen grabbed my wrist and wrenched me from Aaron's grasp. "Is she yours?" Rowen asked, stepping into his space, nearly nose to nose, though Rowen had a few inches on him.

"She isn't property," Aaron told my stepbrother with a flat face.

Rowen looked at me. "Is that true?"

I was drunk on lust and alcohol, and Rowen was my only relief. I needed him badly, and I wasn't sure if we were even going to make it to the car.

I shook my head, and he smiled triumphantly. "Who do you belong to, kitten?"

The sound of my nickname made my stomach flutter. "You," I answered.

"Good girl," he praised.

Despite what our words might have implied, Rowen didn't look at me like property. He looked at me with all the care in the world, like I was something precious and untouchable, something he cherished and worshiped.

So what if he also fucked me like I was just a toy he wanted to ruin?

I was everything to him.

I didn't care that people were watching, listening, probably even judging. All I cared about was getting home as soon as possible so I could be under Rowen for the rest of the night.

"Bernard is outside," he told me without looking away from his enemy. "Go to the car and wait for me."

"Row—"

"Now, Avery." He left no room for argument, his voice sharp and uncompromising.

My legs moved, navigating the crowd until I reached the doors. The cool night air was like a slap in the face, sobering and dizzying all at once.

Bernard was waiting next to the car, pulling open the door the moment he spotted me.

"Good night, miss?" he asked, but I didn't respond as I slid inside.

The door closed, and the quiet that greeted me was heavy. I pressed my forehead against the cool glass and took a few deep breaths, wishing my heart would stop pounding so hard, wishing I could think about anything other than him.

Rowen.

The way he looked at the guy, whose name I'd already forgotten, who dared shoot his shot with me—it wasn't jealousy. It was violent possession that had no boundaries.

And I wanted all of it.

His hands.

His obsession.

His love.

Someone appeared at the door. I leaned away to see my 'owner' looking behind him as he opened the door and slid inside. He looked tense, upset, but when his eyes met mine, it all melted away.

"Avery," he spoke softly.

"Rowen." My voice was barely above a whisper.

I looked down and gasped. Rowen's knuckles were bleeding.

"It's nothing," he said, but he still let me pull his hands to my chest so I could hug them better.

"Did you hit him?" I kept staring at him, a part of me aroused at the idea that he'd hurt someone for me.

Instead of answering the question we both already knew, he pulled me into his lap until I was straddling him and grabbed my face with both hands.

"I love you." He pulled me down to him, crashing our lips together.

11
Rowen

My lips were swollen and tingling by the time Bernard dropped us off, but it was hard to peel myself away from her, even just to get her upstairs to our apartment.

She giggled when we stumbled into the elevator, losing her composure when I dropped my keycard.

"How much did you drink, Avery?"

Her movements were slow and overly exaggerated as she held up two fingers—one from each hand. "Only two."

"Someone doesn't hold their liquor well," I teased as we got off on our floor.

"I don't drink often," she said while I opened the door. "I'm usually a pretty good girl. I don't do bad things." She batted her eyelashes innocently, and my cock strained painfully at the sight.

Fucking hell.

We were barely inside when I wrapped my hand around her throat and used her body to shut the door.

Her kissed-swollen lips parted on a gasp. Her eyes, dazed and wide, locked on mine as if I was the only thing she could see, like everything else had faded away to just this. Just *us*.

Good.

I grabbed her hair—not hard enough to hurt, but hard enough to feel it. My hand on her throat tightened until I could feel her pulse under my thumb.

"I guess I corrupted the good girl, didn't I? Big, bad stepbrother took advantage of the sweet, innocent little stepsister?"

She nodded, a playful smirk forming.

"Did you like it when that man flirted with you? *Touched* you?" My anger was creeping in with the memory of watching another guy lay his hands on her.

"No," she said shaking her head with a pout of her lips.

My fury dissolved as her thighs pressed together, a futile attempt to ease something only *I* could touch.

"You're mine," I told her seriously, planting kisses on her chest and neck. "From the second I laid eyes on you, even though you hated me." I licked her jawline, making her gasp. "You might not survive the love I have for you, Avery." She was whimpering, her need growing. "I'm going to wreck you until there's nothing left."

"Please," she whispered.

"Please, what?" I arched an eyebrow.

"Please fuck me. I can't take it anymore." She tried to move from the door, closer to mine, but I held her steady. "Rowen, *please*."

I leaned close to her ear. "Run, little kitty."

I released her, and she stood frozen for a moment. It was just barely too dark to make out her expression. Then, she ran past me, down the hall, toward the bedrooms.

I took my time shrugging off my jacket, unbuttoning my sleeves and rolling them to my elbows before walking down the hall at a leisurely pace, my hands in my pockets as I whistled to the tune of a pop song Avery had been playing on repeat for the last week.

I couldn't hear her, so I assumed she was hiding already. I decided to start in our bedroom, at the end of the hall, and work my way back to the rest of the apartment.

It was empty, though. No slutty little stepsister to be found.

I went into the closet and shoved a couple of items into my pocket. *Time for a little fun, kitty.*

"Do you really think you can hide from me?" I asked when I stepped back into the hall.

As I stepped into the next room, my makeshift home office, I unbuckled my belt and ripped it from the loops, the whoosh of air loud in the silence. I looked under the desk and in the closet.

Nothing.

I folded my belt in half and snapped it loudly once I reached the hall, knowing the loud crack would make my girl jump.

"When I get my hands on you, the first thing I'm gonna do is spank you with my belt. Why, you ask?" I snapped the belt again. "Because you didn't tell that stupid man to back the fuck off the moment he spoke to you. You kept talking to him, Av. You knew he was flirting, baby. Why didn't you tell him you weren't interested?"

I took a deep breath to calm myself down, remembering I'd already punched the dude hard enough to break his nose before getting kicked out. After Avery walked out, I let him have it, telling him to keep his hands off women who didn't belong to him. He was choking on his blood when they yanked me off him.

The fucker was lucky Avery was waiting in the car for me, ready to go home so I could use her all night.

"Were you trying to make me jealous?" I smirked as I reached the next guest bedroom, stopping when I saw her foot sticking out from under the bed. "Did you want to get me riled up so I'd bring you home and fuck you so hard, you'd never dare let another man flirt with you?" I opened the closet, pretending to look for her. "I bet you were wet thinking about all the things you wanted me to do to you while he yapped. Thinking about how badly you wanted your stepbrother to use that dirty little cunt."

I stopped at the side of the bed and grabbed her ankle. She yelped and kicked, trying to get away, but I yanked her out from under the bed and flipped her over. My knees were on either side of her hips, straddling her, my hands around her throat, squeezing hard enough to make her gasp for each breath. Her body flailed in an attempt to buck me off, but I had something to prove.

"Stop fighting me, kitten."

It took her a few seconds, but she stopped kicking her legs, and her hands quit trying to pull mine from her throat. She lay still, gasping against my palms, her eyes pleading.

"Good girl," I praised, rewarding her with a little more room to breathe. "Stay."

I lifted off her body and left one hand on her throat as I pulled her dress up over her hips, and yanked the top down under her breasts, letting them pop free.

I grabbed the belt I'd dropped on the floor and held it up, tilting my head as my eyes trailed from her face to her breasts.

"No, Row—"

Crack!

She screamed when the leather snapped against her breast, just under her nipple. A red welt appeared within seconds.

"I said I was going to use my belt on you, Av."

Before she could speak, I brought the belt down on her other breast, making her cry out again.

"Fuck," I drew out as I admired the two red marks. Satisfied, I tossed the belt aside. "You're a dirty little slut, getting turned on by that."

"I didn—"

I shoved two fingers inside her and brought them up to show her, the moon reflecting off her juices. "Look. At. That. Seems like someone's lying." A smirk formed on my face as I sucked my fingers clean, moaning as her taste exploded on my tongue. "Fuck. I need more."

I let go of her entirely and slid down her body until my head was between her thighs. My hands held her thighs open as I descended, lapping at her pussy until I found her clit. I sucked it into my mouth, biting down hard enough to make her back arch. I continued to play with it, tugging and sucking until she was ready. I refused to stop, burying two fingers inside of her until she was screaming.

"Rowen! Stop! I can't hold it!" she begged, but I didn't stop.

Not when she clenched down on my fingers.

Not when her thighs trembled.

Not even when there was a hot, sudden rush against my tongue.

I kept going, holding her in place, tongue still moving, swallowing her down like it was my last fucking meal. She writhed under me, still trying to get away, trying to run from the pleasure her body needed.

I pulled back just enough to look at her. Her eyes were wide, shocked, as she took in the sight of me dripping with her, smiling like a deranged beast.

"I love when you do that," I told her, kissing her inner thigh before diving in for more.

12
Avery

Rowen was unreal, going down on me until I squirted all over his face, only to go back for more.

I was screaming and moaning and choking while he devoured me until I was shaking through another orgasm, white-hot pleasure shooting through every nerve, fireworks exploding behind my eyelids.

"Rowen, *please*," I begged.

He was chuckling as he rose above me, and I watched in awe as he removed his shirt, revealing the ink and scars on his body.

It wasn't a view I got often—*all* of him. Rowen usually kept his clothes on, unable to spare the time to get them off before burying himself inside me.

"Fucking Christ..." I muttered, practically drooling over the sex god hovering above me. I wanted to taste him, to lick his abs and suck his nipples. I wanted to cover him with me, make him yearn for me the way I did for him.

"Like what you see?" he asked, using the shirt to clean his face off.

My cheeks burned, embarrassed he'd been down there for *that*. I nodded as he planted his hands on either side of me, his face right above mine. His eyes dipped to my mouth before he came crashing down, kissing me like he owned every goddamn breath.

"Get on the fucking bed," he said when he came up for air. "Ass up."

When he stood, I moved quickly, climbing onto the bed on all fours and lowering my face to the comforter. His hands dug into my hips, dragging me back to the edge of the bed. He remained standing and positioned his cock at my entrance, pushing only an inch or two inside.

"Fuck me already," I growled, trying to rock my hips against him, demanding more.

He held me steady with a bruising grip. "Not yet."

I groaned and shoved my face into the bed.

Then, I heard it.

The click of a cap opening.

I gasped when the cold lube dripped down my crack to my asshole, where his finger was waiting to press inside. Shame burned through me when I moaned.

"It feels good, doesn't it?" he said, taunting me for enjoying something so dirty. "Who knew my stepsister would love her ass played with so much?"

I shivered when his finger retreated, but they were quickly replaced with something else—a small plug. He was patient with my body, slowly fucking me with the toy until I stretched around it.

"Tell me who owns you, Avery," he demanded. "I want to hear you say it before you beg for your stepbrother's cock."

Rowen didn't care how desperate I was.

He wanted reassurance, needed to know his claim over me hadn't somehow disappeared.

It didn't matter if I gave it to him a thousand times. He'd want it a thousand more.

"You, Rowen. I belong to you." I was moaning, trying to fight his hold, get him inside me. My ass was pulsing, pussy clenching around the head of his cock.

"Now beg for it."

"Rowen—"

"Say it, little kitty," he murmured dangerously. "You know what I want to hear."

My skin flushed. No matter how many times I said it, it was still humiliating. Filthy. *Wrong.*

It also made my pulse race and my thighs clench.

"Please..." My voice cracked with desperation. "I need my step-brother's cock. Please, Rowen."

He growled, more animalistic than I'd ever heard, like the dirty words unlocked something feral inside him. "Such a fucking slut for me."

And he thrust into me with one rough stroke that made my soul leave my fucking body.

"You." *Thrust.* "Take." *Thrust.* "My." *Thrust.* "Cock." *Thrust.* "So." *Thrust.* "Well." *Thrust.*

He continued talking, pressing against the plug with the rhythm of his cock, but my ears were filled with my moans as a fire exploded in my veins. My entire body lit up and clenched as another orgasm ripped through me. My lungs refused to draw breath, my eyes glued shut.

I could only endure the ridiculous force of pleasure surging through my body while Rowen continued to fuck me like a mad-man.

"Your cunt is squeezing me," he groaned. "It feels so fucking good knowing your body doesn't want to let me go. You fucking love my cock, don't you? Goddamn, Avery." He paused to growl like a terrifying beast. "Your ass is full. Your stepbrother's cock is inside you, and you're moaning while you come for me." He slammed into me harder. "So fucking perfect."

My mouth wouldn't work, wouldn't beg him for mercy, beg him to let up a little. While he always fucked me hard, he'd never taken me like this, like he had something to prove, something to teach me.

I knew I would feel this for days.

He groaned, and his pace stuttered just enough to warn me what was coming. Rowen didn't pull out, though. He kept thrusting into me until he came, his cum making everything hot and slick. Once his cock started to soften, he finally stopped thrusting.

His body fell over mine, pushing us both onto the bed and pinning me under his body weight for several seconds. It was exactly what I needed, though. Feeling him all around me, holding me down, his smell surrounding me—it brought me back down to Earth.

When he rolled off me, his arms found their way around me and pulled my body to his. We remained like that for a while, letting our hearts and breaths find the same rhythm. I had nearly nodded off when he got up.

He gathered me into his arms and carried me to the shower, where he washed my body and hair. After drying me off, he tucked us into *our* bed.

I wasn't sure if I was dreaming or not when I heard him speak one last time before my eyes closed for good.

"You are *mine*, Av," he whispered firmly and then kissed my temple. "No one will ever take you from me. I'll make sure of that."

13
Rowen

She was so sexy.

Dancing just for me.

In the middle of the club.

Each sway of her hips matched the beat of the music.

She was smiling at me as her hands roamed over the red lace lingerie set she wore. Her fingers flirted with the hem, teasing me.

"Do you love me, Rowen?" she asked.

Before I could answer, Avery stopped dancing, freezing in the middle of the dance floor, arms at her sides, expressionless.

Then, he appeared.

The goddamn man from the bar.

I tried to stand, walk over to her, but I was stuck, unable to move or even yell.

My heart wrenched when his hands wrapped around her waist, trailing up to squeeze her tits before pulling her hair to the side so he could kiss her neck.

The worst part?

She fucking moaned.

Avery closed her eyes as the man kissed her neck then up to her ear and jaw. She turned her head and pressed her lips to his.

I wanted to throw up, watching his tongue enter her mouth.

It had to be a dream—a nightmare—but I couldn't convince myself to wake up. I couldn't do anything. I was trapped.

The man pulled the red lace over her head, leaving her naked, then bent her over the couch.

He looked right at me as he said, "Did you really think a woman like her would stay with a man like you? You're not good enough for her. She deserves so much better."

He grabbed her hair and pulled her head up so she was looking right at me. Her lips were parted on a gasp, eyes heavy-lidded and full of desire.

Please don't let him do it, Av. Don't do this to me. Don't make me watch this.

I tried to talk to her, ask her why she was torturing me, why she was letting another man have her, but I couldn't.

The man thrusted forward, and she groaned erotically. Her eyes squeezed shut, and her face pinched with pleasure.

"Fuck! Yes!" she continued to cry out as he slammed into her. "I'm com—"

I shot up, covered in sweat.

Avery stirred beside me, still sleeping, looking absolutely breathtaking. Her hair had fallen into her face, covering half of it. Her eyelids twitched like she was dreaming. Her slightly parted lips held a small smile.

So peaceful.

My chest was still tight, my lungs refusing to function as the dream still rattled my brain. It felt so real. Too fucking real.

He touched her, made her moan, all while she looked me in the eyes.

And I was powerless to do anything. I could only watch.

I wiped a hand down my face and sighed, wishing I could scrub the image from my mind. The sound of her screaming for *him* still played in my ears, making my stomach twist until I felt sick.

Avery shifted again, murmuring something softly in her sleep.

I froze, afraid she'd wake up and see what a mess I was, that she'd finally figure out I wasn't good enough for her. In that tiny, dark corner of my mind, I knew she deserved better. She just hadn't realized it yet.

I moved to sit on the edge of the bed, elbows resting on my knees, wishing my fears weren't so fucking loud. My jaw clenched tight like it always did when my mind spiraled.

I knew I was intense. I was too much. Not what she *should* want.

But she was in *my* bed.

Willingly.

My chest ached with emotion. I loved her. God, I loved this woman so much, it made me a little unhinged. So much so that I knew if she ever walked away, I'd burn the fucking world to ash just to find her and drag her back with me.

But those three little words hadn't left her lips. Not once.

I'd given them to her again and again, but every time I told her how I felt, she got quiet, like she didn't hear me.

We both knew she did.

I brushed my knuckles down her arm, savoring the touch, no matter how light.

I needed more time with her, just like this.

Silence. Us. Uninterrupted by the world.

I grabbed my phone off the nightstand and walked from the room, hating to leave her for even one second, but I had to know if James had any news for me.

He picked up after four rings. "Hello?" he answered in a sleepy voice.

"Did you get it?" I asked him.

"Good morning to you too," he muttered.

"James..." I didn't have time for his bullshit. I needed answers.

"Let me check my emails," he grumbled.

I walked back to the room silently, peeking around the doorframe to make sure she was still in bed. She hadn't moved.

"They accepted your offer," James said as I moved down the hall to avoid waking Avery. "Said they could be out by the end of the w—"

"Do what it takes to get them out by the end of the day," I snapped.

"I doubt—"

"Whatever it takes, James. Pay for the movers and everything. Avery and I will leave after she wakes up. Make sure they're gone by the time we arrive."

"Got it, boss."

I hung up and then logged onto my laptop to send some emails out, needing everything in order before she woke up.

She wasn't going to be happy about what I'd done, not at first, but she'd eventually understand I only did what was necessary to protect us.

14
Avery

I woke up to an empty bed.

The sheets smelled like him—woodsy and leather. The room was quiet. The curtains still blocked the morning light from invading the dim room.

I lied still for a moment, blinking at the ceiling, letting the fog of sleep fade before sitting upright and throwing my legs over the edge of the bed.

My body ached, raw and bruised deep inside me. The way he'd fucked me the night before could only be described as thorough and unapologetic.

My thighs shook just thinking about it.

And all because of the asshole at the club who couldn't take a hint. I knew it bothered Rowen that I let the guy flirt with me, but I imagined he saw red when the dude grabbed me, trying to pull me away from my stepbrother.

It should've scared me, should've made me question everything when Rowen got into the car with the evidence of what he'd done on his knuckles.

I'd never felt more alive, because the hands he'd used to hurt another man were the same ones taking me to heaven right after.

I reached for my phone on the nightstand to find out I'd slept in a bit.

I hadn't woken up to an empty bed since I figured out Rowen was Michael. He was usually awake before me, but he never left—he just stared at me until I woke up.

I stood from the bed, put on my robe, and walked down the hallway.

A few paces before I reached the common area, I heard his voice.

"She'll be awake any minute now, James." His voice was a quiet growl, like he was frustrated but trying to keep from yelling. "Tomorrow isn't good enough. *Tonight*. We'll be there by ten, and I don't want to see a trace of their existence."

I rounded the corner and leaned on the doorframe, crossing my arms.

He hadn't noticed me yet. He stood near the balcony doors, his hand in his hair, frowning. It didn't matter that he was upset; he was still hot as fuck. His hair was messy, and I'd grown to like the way he'd let his facial hair grow out. It made him look more mature, more tempting.

His demeanor softened when he noticed me in the room. He barked another order at James, telling him not to fuck it up or else, and then tossed his phone to the couch.

His footsteps were desperate, closing the distance between us in no time. His hands grabbed at my face, holding me tight as he slammed his mouth to mine, stealing my breath. I tried to keep up with his vigorous kiss, but it was impossible. I could barely remain upright when he finally released me, his eyes full of a bright emotion I hadn't seen before.

"I have a surprise," he said excitedly.

His smile was contagious.

"What is it?"

"Pack a bag, baby. Anything you might need for a couple of days." He pointed down the hall. "The clothes you ordered arrived early this morning. I snuck them into the closet while you were asleep, so pick out what you want to bring."

He walked down the hallway to his bedroom, leaving me speechless.

"Okay then," I said to myself before turning on my heels and following him, wondering what diabolical plan he'd cooked up.

Nothing was off limits when it came to my stepbrother. I'd learned that the hard way.

"I set a couple of my favorite outfits to the side for you to pack," he stated when I walked into the room.

He was packing a suitcase with his own clothes, folding everything neatly before placing it in the bag. He gestured to the suitcase next to his.

"This one's yours, baby."

I walked over to him, and he kissed my forehead before disappearing into the bathroom. The outfits he'd picked were cute—shorts and shirts that I'd picked out but he'd coordinated. I put them in my suitcase.

"Where are we going?" I asked when he returned to the room with more stuff to pack.

"Ah, ah, you won't get answers out of me that easily." He continued packing. "Don't you know what a surprise is?"

I studied him with narrow eyes, hoping he'd crack, but he was steady, smirking at my futile attempts to unlock answers.

"How long are we going to be gone? What if I need something I don't bring?"

"I can get whatever you need delivered to us." He zipped his luggage. "Whatever you need, whatever you want." His eyes scanned my suitcase. "Almost done? The car is outside for us."

I thought for a moment. "Let me grab a few more things."

Ten minutes later, Rowen was loading our bags into the trunk of a silver luxury car, telling me he couldn't wait to see my face when he revealed the big secret.

"Don't you dare touch that handle," he commanded, gently pushing me out of the way so he could open the passenger door for me.

Before I could get into the car, he threaded one of his hands into my hair and pulled my face to his, pressing our lips together in a gentle, consuming kiss, branding me with the taste of him.

"I love you," he whispered as he rested his forehead against mine. "I love you so fucking much it hurts, Av."

Instead of waiting for me to reply like usual, he pulled away and let me get inside the car without another word.

When he sat in the driver's seat, he put his hand on my knee before easing onto the street with a smile on his face.

What has you smiling like that, mister?

15
Rowen

"No." Her arms were crossed over her chest.

Turned out, Avery wasn't the type of girl who liked to be surprised with a big move to a new house without consulting her first. She'd finally managed to wear me down a few hours into the road trip, and I confessed everything.

I squeezed her thigh, one hand still on the wheel. "You haven't even seen the place yet. It's beautiful."

"So you say, but what if I hate it?"

I look over at her. "You won't. I had James comb through your Pinterest. He said you were quite thorough in the board titled 'Dreamy Home Goals'. It didn't take him long to figure out what you'd like best. Within a few hours, the owners accepted our offer."

"*Our* offer?" she said sarcastically. "And I don't care if James stalked my fucking Pinterest. There's no way—"

She stopped talking when I handed her my phone, pictures of our new home pulled up.

The house was everything I wanted.

Private. Remote. The kind of place no one would stumble upon or find easily unless they were meant to. It was hidden deep in the woods—nothing but trees and sky for miles in every direction.

No neighbors. No traffic. No noise. Just us.

Our new home was everything she wanted too.

Luxury log cabin.

There were three guest bedrooms—and I already knew what I wanted to fill them with.

The three identical bathrooms were sleek and modern, with natural stone accents, warm lighting, and freestanding tubs.

There was an office in the corner wing, perfect for me—and for spreading her over my desk when I needed a break.

The kitchen was oversized and high-end, and it would be fully stocked in the morning with everything I planned to make for her. I could already see her, barefoot and wearing my shirt, sitting on the counter—my little taste tester.

There were two living rooms, one for guests and one for her to lounge in.

And the master bedroom?

It was massive, with two walk-in closets and an impressive primary bath with a jacuzzi tub and shower open to the outdoors. I already had a special bed frame on the way, perfect for everything I planned to do to her.

And the porch. It wrapped around the whole house, with rocking chairs and thick wooden beams. It was the perfect place to watch her enjoy the sunrise or bend her over the railing at dusk.

I also ordered a hot tub that would be there in the morning. A big one, just for us. The final touch.

The cost was immense, but I didn't blink. This house was where I planned to build her a life so private, so perfect, she'd never dream of leaving it.

Or me.

We'd spend every day making up for the time we never had.

"It really is beautiful," she said quietly in the passenger seat.

"Told you," I said smugly.

"Doesn't excuse the fact that you went behind my back." She paused, still scrolling pictures. "How did you even manage this overnight?"

"I can be quite persuasive, baby." I smiled, rubbing my thumb on her thigh, loving the way she felt, wishing we were closer to our new home so I could feel *more* of her. "You have the rest of the drive to shop for the house. Furniture, decor, anything you want."

She looked as if she didn't believe me. "Row...I can't spend more of your money like that."

I pulled over on the side of the road and turned to face her. "It's our money, Av. The only reason I ever wanted to make it big was to give you the life you deserved." I took one of her hands and kissed it. "Let me spoil you. Let me give you everything you want."

"I—"

"If you want to continue this argument, you can get out of the car right now and run into the woods over there. I'll fuck you until you agree to drain my bank account, and then I'll drag you back to the car and take you home just to fuck you again to christen it."

She squirmed in her seat, but her wide eyes never left mine. My gaze dropped to her lips, watching her tongue skirt across them.

"Have I made myself clear?" I asked her, ignoring her obvious signs of lust, hoping it would continue to build on our drive until she couldn't keep her hands off me.

She nodded slowly, accepted my phone, and started shopping. Once I confirmed she was adding things to the cart, I pulled back onto the road and gripped her upper thigh hard, reminding her I was watching.

16
Avery

He was fucking crazy.

I honestly couldn't believe I'd just gone along with it instead of demanding he take me back to the apartment, but any desire to do so faded to nothing when we finally pulled up to the house.

The pictures didn't do its beauty justice. The warm porch lights made the logs stand out, giving them a welcoming glow. There was a pair of rocking chairs on one side, making the house seem cozy.

It really was my dream home.

"Oh my God..."

"Like it?" Rowen asked smugly.

I fought rolling my eyes when he got out of the car and walked around to help me out. "I still don't understand why you did this," I said as he led me to the front door, his hand on my back.

He pulled out his phone, and after he tapped the screen, the door lock clicked.

"I want to give you the world, Avery." He pulled me close and kissed the top of my head. "Just enjoy it, okay? Don't overthink it."

The paranoid voices in my head faded to silence as he took my hand and reached for the doorknob so we opened the door together.

The butterflies in my stomach multiplied by a hundred.

He loved me so much, he bought a fucking house for me.

Why couldn't I tell him I felt the same way?

"I know I probably should've waited to bring you here until all our stuff was moved, but I was too excited," he admitted as we walked through the entryway and into a large room. "It's gonna look even better when you decorate, baby."

I smiled at him and lifted to my toes to kiss his cheek. "Don't you want to help decide what it looks like?"

He shook his head. "I want what you want. I can make my office my own little space." His eyebrows rose. "Unless you want that room too?"

"You're impossible," I muttered, even though I was smiling.

I yawned, tired from our long drive, and he chuckled. "You can't be tired yet. I need to fill this house with your screams, kitten."

"Can't wait until tomorrow?" I teased, already walking away to look around.

Before I made it to what looked like the kitchen, Rowen threw me over his shoulder, carrying me down a dark hallway and up some stairs. He opened a door, and I was thrown onto a soft mattress.

While I was tired, my body *needed* Rowen, so I wasn't about to complain about having sex with him. My core still ached from the rough fuck the night before, but there was an even deeper ache within me for an entirely different reason.

"The bed frame won't be here until tomorrow, but you better believe I'm going to make love to you on our new mattress before I let you fall asleep."

His voice was deep and desperate, rough in all the sexy ways. He was grinding himself into me, his hard cock making itself known behind his clothes.

"Rowen," I moaned when he sucked on my neck, grazing my skin with his teeth.

"Beg for me," he demanded. "Beg for my cock. Tell me how bad you want it, Av."

"I want your cock, Rowen. Please fuck me." I grabbed the bottom of his shirt and helped him get it over his head, tossing it somewhere off the bed. "I need you inside me."

I wasn't confident with my dirty talk, but the way he growled at my filthy words gave me a confidence boost.

Rowen lifted the hem of my sundress and moved down until his head was between my legs. He grabbed my panties, pulling them off me gently as he kissed my inner thighs until they were trembling.

"Hands," he said impatiently.

I put my wrists together for him, and he tied them with my panties.

He lifted my bound wrists above my head and said, "Stay, or I won't let you come."

His threat sent shudders down my spine, and I struggled to stay still as he kissed and nipped his way between my legs. My hips instantly bucked against him when his tongue flattened against my clit. Fingers invaded my entrance, curling to stroke a spot that made my toes curl.

"Fuck, Row..." I trembled as he worked my clit with his tongue and started fucking me with his fingers.

My reaction was the encouragement he needed to work even harder, faster, until my stomach tightened. I recognized a familiar feeling and panicked.

"Stop. Wait."

He ignored me and pressed his free hand down on my stomach. I tried to hold it in, refuse to give him what he was trying to force from me, but it was inevitable, and within seconds, I was coating my thighs as I screamed his name.

Every muscle in my body was strained. My eyes squeezed shut. I had to hold on to the sheets to keep my hands above my head like I was supposed to. Rowen was groaning, pleased as I soaked us both with my orgasm, pulling more from me with each thrust of his fingers.

"Rowen, please. Fuck. Please stop," I begged, unable to put much strength behind my words, still drowning in pleasure.

He didn't stop when my orgasm was over; he just continued to force more spasms from me as I cried for mercy.

Just before I thought I was going to come again, he pulled away. My body sagged, and I was aware—and self-conscious—of the puddle under me. Rowen clearly didn't give a single fuck, because he crawled over me, lined his cock with my entrance, and thrusted into me.

"I'll never get tired of the way you feel around me, Av. Who knew my stepsister would have such an amazing cunt?" he groaned, moving inside me like he needed to claim every inch even though I was thoroughly his already. "Just look at you. So wet. So perfect."

My legs wrapped tightly around his waist, and I fought the urge to bury my fingers in his hair. I bit his shoulder as he filled me over and over, the steady, controlled strokes sending my eyes to the back of my head.

"Fuck, I could stay inside you forever," he rasped, grinding his hips harder, just enough to make me cry out. "I love you like this, open and desperate for me."

I couldn't say anything back. I could barely breathe. My body was still twitching from the last orgasm. His body was hot and heavy on top of mine, and his hard thrusts turned my brain off. Despite being overstimulated and gasping for breath, I still needed more, caught in the space between begging for mercy and for pleasure.

"Row—I can't. Too much—"

"No, Av. You can take it." He caught my chin between his fingers, tilting my face so I had to look at him. His eyes were burning with an intensity that shook me to my core. "You were made for this. For me."

He leaned down until his lips grazed my ear, making me shiver. His thrusts grew stronger, each jerk of his hips having its own purpose.

I could feel myself losing the battle, my thighs shaking, my stomach coiling with heat and need. The pressure was growing, spiraling.

"I'm going to fill you up. Keep you so full of me. Wreck you until you can't think straight between the breaks from my cock inside you." His voice had dropped to a rough whisper. "We'll fill every room with babies. *Our* babies."

My breath caught, and my eyes snapped open. My brain was startled by his words, clawing its way out of the lusty haze to argue with him, but my body didn't hesitate. My pussy clenched around him as a broken moan escaped my lips.

I heard him curse, and his thrusts slowed a bit, but the passion behind them didn't.

I should have been alarmed. His words were sudden and intense, but they forced a picture into my head: him holding me from behind in our new kitchen, one hand splayed across my swollen belly.

My vision blurred as I whimpered—helpless and wrecked.

He must've felt it too.

"You *want* that, don't you? Fuck, your pussy is begging for my cum, wanting every last drop."

I was sobbing, broken under the intensity of the moment. "I—fuck—Rowen, plea—"

I was too far gone to pretend the idea of him filling me up again and again didn't turn me on, didn't scratch some deep desire to be his, even more than I already was.

"Just like that," he rasped, his voice strained with need.

He groaned like he was coming undone, and his hips stuttered until I felt the heat of his cum rush into me, filling me up. I could feel it seep out onto my thighs with each rough thrust, but he didn't stop to worry about the mess.

After he fucked me through all the aftershocks of my orgasm, he stilled. I waited for him to pull out, but he didn't. He stayed inside me, staring down at me with a terrifying expression.

"I wasn't lying, Av," he said quietly, but his words still boomed in my ears. "I want to see your belly swollen with my babies, enough to fill the house with the pitter-patter of little feet and high-pitched giggles. I've never wanted anything more."

I shook my head, knowing I was not in my right mind to have this conversation. My ovaries were screaming for him, begging to bring his desires to fruition, more than willing to do their part to make it happen.

"I don't th—"

"Shh," he said before pressing his lips to mine with a gentleness I didn't know he was capable of. "We don't have to talk about it now. There's plenty of time. I just wanted to be honest with you."

Somehow, that was comforting, knowing it was just sweet words he'd expressed, not something he genuinely wanted right this second. While I still believed kids were the last thing we needed, I would have been lying if I said the idea was totally revolting.

He'd invaded my brain and planted the seed, and I knew I'd probably eventually give in to him.

Plus, the idea of a little version of him running around didn't sound *that* awful.

17
Rowen

Her eyes were open when I rolled over, staring at me, her cheek half-buried in the pillow, breathing softly.

I blinked, giving my vision a moment to adjust to the morning light filtering in through unfamiliar curtains.

Our new house.

Our new bedroom.

Last night came rushing back. The shocked gasp when I pulled into the driveway. The way her hands trembled when we opened the front door. The silence that settled as she walked inside.

The way she broke open for me in our bed.

I'd been ready with the new mattress and waterproof sheets.

Best investment ever.

And like the good girl she was, she soaked the sheets, screaming my name until her voice broke.

I laid her back down on the bed after replacing the sheets, but by the time I'd returned from tossing them in the wash, she was out cold, so I crawled in beside her and fell asleep to the sound of her deep breaths.

Her eyes traced my face like she was trying to memorize it. I couldn't tell whether she wanted to kiss me or cry.

My confession during sex had startled her, even if she did clench around my cock the moment I told her my ultimate goal. When she'd brought it up after, I tried my best to cover it up, claiming I was just caught up in the moment, that there was time to discuss such things.

That seemed to be enough for her, but I almost felt bad for lying.

"Are you okay?" Her brows were scrunched with concern.

My hand found her waist, brushing my thumb over the curve of her hip. "Of course, baby. Are you okay?"

She took a second before nodding slowly. Her lips parted like she was about to say something, but nothing came out.

"Avery, you're looking at me like I scared you." I kissed her forehead and pulled her into my body. "Or like you want to start planning the wedding. I honestly can't tell which."

She giggled, but it was half-hearted. "Last night was just…a lot."

I waited for more.

"I wasn't expecting you to… I didn't know you…" She squeezed me like I was her lifeline. "Did you mean what you said?"

"I said a lot of things."

She sighed. "About getting me…pregnant."

I tucked my fingers under her chin and lifted until she was looking at me. "Every fucking word."

Her breath hitched, and I could see the moisture pooling in her eyes.

I wasn't sure I was going to give her a choice in the matter, but I still wondered what went through her head when she thought about having a baby with the stepbrother she used to despise. I was too afraid to ask, though, afraid to know the truth—that she might not want that, want me, at all.

For me, I couldn't wait to see Avery pregnant, holding a baby, singing soft lullabies to our children as they fell asleep.

Our perfect little family.

A single tear fell from her eye, but I didn't try to catch it as it cascaded down her cheek and onto my chest.

"We don't have to talk about anything until you're ready," I assured her.

She nodded and tucked herself back against me, placing her hand over my heart like she wanted to reach in and take it.

I'd let her. Avery owned my entire being. She didn't understand the lengths I'd go to keep everything perfect for us, to keep us together.

But I couldn't risk scaring her off now, when nothing was tying us together. Even just the thought of losing Avery made my heart ache.

"How does breakfast sound?" I asked her, needing to get out of bed, needing something to focus my energy on.

"I could eat," she offered.

Once downstairs, Avery started looking around the house, opening doors and walking through the rooms while I busied myself in the kitchen.

"This house is amazing," she said once she finished her tour.

"So it has your approval?"

She rolled her eyes. I put my hands on her hips and dragged her body to mine.

"Come on, baby," I murmured against her lips, teasing her, enjoying the way she chased me. "Just admit you love the house so we can move on."

"You shou—"

"Next time, I'll ask you before I do anything crazy like this, okay? I promise."

Her eyes searched mine, looking for something. "Fine," she finally admitted. "I do like the house."

"Just like?" I asked as I dug my fingers into her ribs, making her laugh. "I spent all this money on a house you *like*?"

She tried to talk, but she was laughing too hard to get any words out. When I let up, she said, "I love it. It's unbelievable, but I love it. It's everything I dreamed about."

"It's all yours, Av," I said before dipping to press our mouths together.

She accepted me instantly, parting her lips so my tongue could slip inside. I grabbed the backs of her thighs, her flesh yielding to my grip, and lifted her onto the counter so I could properly consume her.

I refused to let her come up for air, kissing her until she pushed on my chest, begging to breathe. After a few more seconds, I backed away, watching her gasp before diving into her again.

Avery was a drug I couldn't get enough of. She was all I needed to be happy and whole. As long as I had her, nothing could touch me.

18
Avery

Days turned into weeks, then months. Before I knew it, I'd settled into our new life, and three months passed quickly.

Everything was perfect.

The stuff he had me shop for arrived within days of our move, and we spent the following week getting the house just the way we—though Rowen was annoyingly agreeable with everything I said—wanted.

Rowen had only worked outside the home for one day, and he was back by the time I went to bed. Everything else—emails, phone calls, even video meetings—he handled in his office, which happened to be the only room that oozed his personality.

He'd painted the walls a dark blue, a color that complemented the dark wood accents and fireplace. His desk was huge, big enough to lie across—we'd tested it multiple times. His shelves were full of books and pictures of me or us together.

I hadn't cooked a single meal for Rowen. The only time I got my hands on a pan was when he got an important phone call and had to step away, leaving me to man the stove for what seemed like two seconds. He insisted on cooking for me, that it was his *love language*.

Every love language was his love language.

Rowen encouraged me to take online courses if I was interested but that I didn't need to. He assured me our finances would be just fine, so I should choose what made me happy and not what made the most sense. I opted to take another semester off and maybe start up again for the fall semester.

He bought me anything I could have ever wanted and then some. Most of the time, I didn't even ask. There were even a couple of instances when I had searched for something on my phone but never actually ordered it, yet somehow, it appeared a few days later.

He gave me back and foot massages daily—even brushed my hair before bed every night—saying he wanted me happy and relaxed. Those massages usually ended up with us naked, putting our furniture to good use. The woods surrounding us were a huge bonus as well.

"Are you ready, kitten?" he said in my ear, his hands on my bare hips as we stood on the edge of the forest.

The soft rain was cool against my skin, falling down my breasts, running over my nipples, making me shiver.

I nodded, my heart pounding in my chest, scared and thrilled all at once.

"Two minutes." He started going through our rules. "Run as far and as fast as you can. I want you to fight me when I catch you. Don't make it easy, okay?" He kissed my neck. "I want to force you to give in. I want to hear you beg me to stop while I fuck you into the ground. Give me your best, little kitty, and I'll make you see fucking stars."

I forced a swallow, my body shaking with anticipation. Rowen remained behind me, probably loving the way I squirmed uncomfortably.

"Rowen..." I whispered, frustrated, needing our games to begin before I exploded.

He'd made me go three days without an orgasm, edged me multiple times as he laughed sadistically, never letting me cross the finish line.

"Is someone excited?"

Fucking understatement.

If he didn't fuck me soon, *I* was going to be the one chasing *him*. I needed him inside me, using me, more than anything. The bastard had turned me into an addict.

To make matters worse, Rowen was *painted* this time instead of wearing his balaclava. He'd gotten jealous when I liked a video of a man painted to look like a skull with a wide smile. He even copied the black body paint, only leaving one spot uncovered.

My initials.

The only reason we made it out of the house was Rowen's determination to 'use me thoroughly', since I'd been a bit mouthy with all the edging.

"Run," he barked with a low growl.

So, I did.

I took off into the woods, immediately darting to the left up the hill behind our home, knowing that when I was out of Rowen's sight—even though he'd promised not to look—I was going to run to the right.

The ground was different here than back at our parents' house, softer and less rocky. It made it easier to run barefoot. I planned to get to the creek at the bottom of the hill, the one I often saw when we went for sunset walks, but I'd never made it that far when he was after me.

It didn't matter how many times Rowen chased me, how many times he hunted me down and fucked my soul right out of my body. I'd never lose the thrill. It was exhilarating. Running. Hiding. *Fighting*.

Consensual non-consensual had quickly become another favorite kink of ours, especially when he wanted to chase me.

He always carried me back home afterward and treated me like a princess, tending to any minor scrapes I might've gotten, rubbing my sore muscles, and helping me clean the dirt from my body.

"Here, kitty kitty," Rowen yelled as he always did when he topped the hill, signaling the start of the *real* fun.

Both fear and excitement bubbled in my chest, the pressure making me want to burst. My hands were shaking, and even when I stopped for a brief break, I couldn't stop from bouncing on my feet like an excited puppy.

I reached a marked tree and smiled, knowing Rowen was going to love the little surprise I'd planted just for him.

19
Rowen

She thought she could deceive me with her false trail to the left when it was very clear she had gone to the right. I could see the end of her path in the mud to one side, but not the other.

Cute.

"She tried." I chuckled to myself before jogging to the right.

I heard her giddy laughter just ahead, something she had a hard time containing when the excitement was too much for her mind and body to handle.

I followed the sound, weaving through trunks and bushes like I was made for this, pausing ever so often to make sure I was on the right path. The light rain on the leaves was making things a tad harder than usual.

It was also making things messier, the damp ground slowly turning into mud. My new goal had become to make sure Avery was exhausted and filthy by the time we made it back to the house.

A twig snapped, and my head jerked in time to catch a glimpse of her, hair wet and legs pumping as she darted behind a crooked oak tree with a squeal.

Fuck, that sound.

"You're not gonna get away from me, little kitty," I called out, amused and dark with promise. "We both know exactly how this ends."

My pace slowed until I was approaching the tree with caution, knowing the prey behind it was easily spooked. I could already feel her skin, taste her on my tongue, hear her breathy little moans.

My pulse was loud in my ears as I approached the tree then surged forward to catch her off guard.

Only, she was ready for me, and she dashed in the other direction, barely missing my attempt to grab her. She shrieked and laughed at the same time as she sprinted away.

Too soon to celebrate, you little brat.

I took five long steps then lunged at her, tackling her to the wet grass, turning so she landed on me instead of the ground. She squirmed in my grip, but I held her to me, wrapping my arms around her.

"Caught you," I growled before trying to kiss her, but she turned her head. "You'll regret that later."

She looked down with a devilish smile.

Then, I felt it.

A small blade against my throat.

"You're *really* going to regret that."

She shrugged and pushed the knife hard enough to make me hiss, the blade digging into my skin enough to burn. "I don't think you're in any position to be making threats, do you?"

I narrowed my eyes, but I was mesmerized by the fierce look in hers, the way she glowed with victory. She started to wiggle again, but when I dug my fingers into her hips, she pressed the blade harder.

Her smile grew when I released her, and she sat up to straddle me, all while dragging the tip of the blade down my painted torso, stopping at my belly button. My cock twitched in my pants, a painful reminder I shouldn't have been turned on by my woman wielding a knife pointed at my stomach.

"What's your plan, kitten?" My voice was low and taunting, knowing she didn't have it in her to hurt me. "Do you really think you scare me?"

My hands dug into her thighs until she whimpered. Her guard dropped—her body always under my control—so I grabbed her wrists and flipped us over. Now, *I* was the one straddling her, pinning her hands to the forest floor, staring at her parted lips.

I'm her fucking predator.

It would never be the other way around.

I jutted my chin to the knife in her hand.

"What was the plan, Av?" I leaned down until my lips were hovering over hers. "Were you going to hurt me? Cut me maybe?"

She moaned when my hips pressed down, grinding my cock against her.

"Does that turn you on?" I teased her lips with my tongue, pulling back when she tried to kiss me. "Do you want me to bleed for you? Do you want to mark me again?"

Her eyes were wide, her bottom lip tucked between her teeth.

"Answer me," I snapped, my patience wearing thin.

"Yes."

My cock was begging for her pussy, but my heart ached to give her everything she wanted.

"I want you riding my cock while you do it," I said before flipping us back over.

I slipped my sweatpants down until my cock sprang free, and then I helped her lower herself onto me. Her tight cunt felt amazing as she descended, taking me deep. My hands remained on her hips, holding her down even as she tried to bounce.

"Row, it's too much," she whined.

"You can handle it, baby. Stay right there until you're finished carving me up. Then, I want to finish what I started."

"This isn't exactly clea—"

"We can clean it when we get back home; just hurry up before I decide to fuck you instead and you lose your opportunity." I took her hand, placing the end of the blade over a blank spot on my hip.

The rain had washed a decent amount of the paint off my body, but it was still risky to let her do this. It didn't matter. I needed her to understand just how deep I'd fallen for her, how willing I was to do anything for her.

It would help her understand the things I'd done, everything I put her through to get us here.

A sharp pain exploded across my hip as she pressed the knife into my skin. I had no idea what she was carving. It could've been a dick for all I knew, but I savored every slice, every sting, my cock hardening with the pain. I watched her eyebrows knit as she focused, taking her time to give me another mark.

She got upset every time I shifted my hips, moving my cock inside her.

"I'll fuck it up if you don't stay still," she said through gritted teeth.

"Please hurry," I groaned.

She giggled. "It's kind of cute when you beg. Now I get why you like hearing it so much."

"I'll have you begging soon if you don't hurry it up, Av."

I was hanging by a thread, ready to snap at any moment and fuck her no matter the consequence. Even getting stabbed didn't sound all that bad if it meant being buried inside her tight, wet cunt.

"I'm done."

I moved quickly, grabbing the knife from her hand, tossing it somewhere far away from us so she didn't get hurt. Then, I flipped us back over, staying inside her the entire time. She gasped when I started moving, thrusting with deep desperation.

The blood from my new wound was warm as it trickled down my thigh, but it didn't stop me from plowing into her until her eyes rolled back and her pussy clenched, refusing to let me go, begging me to fill her up.

Which was exactly what I did.

Pleasure zipped up my thighs to my balls, and my cock pulsed inside her.

"I fucking love when you take my cum like a good girl," I taunted as I spilled into her, hot and heavy, the sound of skin on skin quickly becoming wetter. "You're such a little whore for your stepbrother, Av. Just look at you. Moaning my name. Writhing under me like a pathetic little animal." I continued thrusting, her orgasm lasting longer than mine, prolonging her pleasure. "You're so desperate for my cock; you'd do anything for it, wouldn't you?"

Her eyes opened, and she nodded.

I could've come again if I'd had it in me, but I was already softening inside her.

Later, I promised us both.

Avery wasn't full enough. She needed my cum dripping out of her for the rest of the day, so I'd be fucking her again as soon as I recovered.

20
Avery

"I said no," he snapped harshly.

"Rowen, you have no idea how they'll react. It's been months. Maybe everything has blown over. Maybe we have to be the ones to take the first step."

"Do you not remember the things they said that night? Disgusting? That we should be ashamed? Or my personal favorite: 'You're not right in the head'?" He mocked his father's voice for the last part.

"It was a heated moment. I can't imagine being in their shoes and walking in on their step kids having sex."

This wasn't the first time we'd argued about seeing our parents. Rowen wanted to cut them off completely, never see them again, pretend like they didn't exist. He took it as a personal hit every time I mentioned going to visit them, as if my wanting to see them meant I didn't want to see him anymore.

"Why do you keep making excuses for them, Av? Who cares what they were going through—we're their fucking kids! They could've taken a step back before saying all that shit. They didn't have to tear us down the moment things got uncomfortable." He was holding my hands in his, gripping them like he was afraid to let go, afraid I'd walk out the door and never come back.

Truth be told, it was my fault he was so upset this time. After so many failed attempts at convincing him we should visit, I'd decided to go on my own—in secret. Rowen wasn't meant to come out and see me trying to lug my suitcase to the garage.

He panicked, thinking I was leaving him, but the real reason hadn't brought him any more comfort.

"Please, Rowen." I looked him in the eyes, making him see how serious I was about doing this. "You can come with me, and if anything goes wrong, we leave. I won't fight or argue. One hateful glance or comment, and we leave." I squeezed his hands. "I want you to come with me."

Rowen didn't cry—not that I was aware of anyway—but he looked like he was about to. He looked like a broken man who'd just lost the fight of his life.

I understood, though. I couldn't imagine the pain of losing him, especially if it was his choice to leave. I just wished he'd give me the benefit of the doubt, understand I missed my mom, even if she did say those awful things to me that night and had ignored me ever since.

"We can't," he said while shaking his head.

"*You* can't," I started to pull away from him, "but I can."

At first, I thought he was going to keep me there, refuse to let me go, because his hands were frozen around mine. Then, his grip loosened, and my hands fell to my sides.

"I'll be back. I promise." I stood on my toes to kiss his lips, but he didn't kiss me back. Guilt settled in my stomach like a brick. I felt like I was going to throw up as I grabbed my suitcase and walked out the door.

The garage was quiet. I put the suitcase in the trunk, but by the time I closed it, I heard his footsteps.

"I'm sorry, Av. I can't let you go."

He threw me over his shoulder and headed back inside.

"Rowen! What are you—Put me down! Right now! Stop this!"

I continued to scream as he carried me through the house, up the stairs, into our bedroom. He tossed me onto the bed, and I couldn't help but giggle.

You should've known he'd want sex before you left.

My stomach fluttered and my thighs clenched. I let him cuff my wrists to the headboard. He didn't say anything, even when he dragged my panties down my legs and lifted my dress to my hips.

His eyes finally met mine as he lowered his head between my legs, kissing up from my knee to my middle on one side, then the other. I was panting by the time he reached my core the second time.

"Please, Rowen," I begged shamelessly.

Instead of indulging me, he kissed the insides of my thighs, avoiding me, ignoring my pleas.

"Fuck..." I mewled.

It hadn't been long since the last time he'd edged me, and this felt just like that.

He was truly evil if that was his plan, edging me before letting me leave. Knowing I wouldn't be able to think about anything except his cock the entire time I was gone, that I'd rush back as soon as possible just to bend over and beg for him.

"Please don't do this." My voice was cracking, breathless, as he continued to kiss the sensitive flesh of my thighs. "Don't leave me hanging, Row."

He growled, still not speaking, as his fingers spread my pussy while his tongue invaded my entrance.

I gasped, my back arching off the bed, eyes closing tightly, as he fucked me with his tongue for a few seconds before moving to flick my clit then returning to fuck me. He did this multiple times, winding my body as tight as it would possibly go.

My skin was coated with sweat, my heart raced erratically, and my toes curled. I writhed under him, but he held on to me, devouring my pussy like he'd never eat it again.

I could feel my orgasm getting closer, and I knew it was going to leave us soaked and require major cleanup afterward. He knew my body like no one else ever could.

"Fuck, Row... I need to c—"

Rowen's mouth left me, leaving me right on the edge. My entire body tingled painfully, my mind stuck between worlds. Everything got fuzzy, and my body cried for relief, but there was none.

My eyes refused to open, but I felt the bed lift where my stepbrother had once lain.

"Rowen?"

I blinked until I could see him, standing over me, looking hurt and angry.

Then, he walked out, and the door clicked shut, leaving me all alone, restrained to the bed, my brain still buffering from the way he'd left me.

No...

21
Rowen

She was going to leave without telling me, sneak out while I was working.

What the fuck did she expect me to do? Let her go when I explicitly said we weren't inviting those people back into our lives?

I rubbed my face with both hands as I stood on our porch, looking out into the woods. Just two days before, I'd chased her down and let her cut into me before I fucked her so hard, I had to carry her back to the house, passed out.

I peered down at the lines she'd carved in the form of a kitten. She'd been a lot more confident with the knife this time, not hesitating or worrying like she did back then.

It honestly looked like a child drew it, but I loved it. Other than her initials, it was my new favorite piece.

But then, she tried to leave.

I could still hear her yelling upstairs, crying and demanding I let her go, through the open windows.

My heart was in my throat.

Didn't she love me?

She hadn't said it, but I'd felt it in the way she kissed me, fucked me, in the way she poured herself into our home, making it the perfect place for us.

I couldn't understand why she'd wanted to leave, but I also refused to let myself spiral. I just had to convince her everything she needed was there, with me.

So, I busied myself in the kitchen, ordered some things online, and once she stopped screaming for me—two hours later—I walked back into our bedroom.

"Av..." I said gently as I approached the bed.

She was a mess, tears running down her face, smearing her makeup. Her hair was no longer in a cute ponytail, her dress bunched up under her breasts.

She'd managed to pull herself up so her back rested against the headboard, but her arms were still up at her sides, her wrists cuffed to the rings attached to our headboard.

"Ro—wen," she sobbed. "W—why did y—you d—do this t—to me?"

My heart sank, and I rushed to her side, sitting on the edge of the bed and putting the plate on the nightstand. I held her face with both hands, wiping her tears and a stray hair from her face.

"Everything's okay, baby." I kissed her forehead. "You scared me. I didn't know what else to do. I thought you were leaving me."

She shook her head. "No. Never."

"I can't lose you." The words were both a confession and a threat, heavy and final.

She watched me carefully, almost afraid, but I could see something else, something dark. She knew why I was like this, loved the way I was for her.

"You make me crazy, Avery." I dragged my hand through my hair with a laugh. "I'm so fucking obsessed with you," I said, my voice lowering with hunger. "I'm not sure who I am anymore. You burned everything down until the only thing left standing was *you*. I can't shut it off, Av. I can't be away from you. I can't—"

My hands started a path down her body, and soon, I was back between her legs, staring up at her. She was still sobbing, but her breathing had changed, as had the look in her eyes.

"You're my everything," I told her as I kissed her thighs. "You should hate me. Maybe you still do. But I can't stop. I can't let you leave. I can't *be* without you."

Her thighs were damp with sweat, but also from her arousal. I'd left her right on the edge earlier, and the evidence coated her inner thighs. Her smell invaded my nose, making my cock ache.

"Please, Rowen," she begged, though I couldn't be sure exactly *what* it was she was asking for.

So, I gave her the thing I was willing to let her have.

Avery was soaked, dripping onto the bed. I cleaned up every last fucking drop with my tongue then picked up where I'd left off last time.

Her thighs trembled as I fucked her with my tongue then played with her clit. I worked her up to the brink of destruction, but just before she erupted, I backed away again.

She was really crying now, tugging at her cuffs, pushing her hips forward to chase my mouth.

"Rowen!" Her throat cracked with her scream.

"It'll feel so good when it finally happens," I spoke in a low voice.

She moaned when I got back to it, but she'd hardly had any time to cool off, so her body tightened within several seconds. Her arms yanked at the cuffs, and she huffed with frustration.

I did the same thing multiple times, until she was growling at me each time I stopped.

"Rowen. Fuck..." Her voice was broken and quiet, like she was barely holding on.

Good.

"Do you want to come, baby?"

She was nodding.

"Words, Av. Tell me with your words."

"Yes. I want to come."

I smiled. "Promise me you won't leave."

Her eyes opened slowly, and she peered down at me between her legs. She seemed to sober at the reminder of her predicament.

"Rowen..." Her lips pressed together. "I need to—"

I cut her off by diving back into her pussy, licking and sucking until she squirmed. The moment I felt her body start to shake, I pulled away.

"Fuck..." she muttered, her eyes closed now.

"I'll let you come if you just say it," I reminded her. "Tell me you won't leave. Promise to stay here, with me."

"I want to see—"

I edged her again.

"Rowen, stop th—"

And again.

"Please stop—"

And again.

"Fine!" she cried out, her voice straining with desperation. "I won't leave, okay? Just let me come. *Please!*"

She gave me what I wanted, earning what she wanted. I shoved two fingers inside her, curling them to stroke that special spot, and sucked on her clit. Within seconds, she was breaking for me, squirting onto my face, soaking the bed, making a beautiful mess.

"I'm done! I'm done!"

She flailed frantically when I kept going, pushing her body further. I continued to torture her, forcing her to give me more.

And even though she claimed she was done, it wasn't long before her pussy clenched around my fingers, squirting once again. She gasped and moaned, her body seizing up to the point she was stiff while the orgasm overtook her.

"I love watching you break for me, little sis," I groaned, keeping my fingers inside her, slowing my pace but keeping her under the haze of sex. "How does that make you feel? Knowing I can make you do anything I want?"

She whimpered.

I withdrew my fingers and sucked them clean, loving the way her taste exploded over my taste buds. My cock was screaming to be let out, to have what was his.

"I'm going to fuck you, and then I'm going to feed you dinner."

I pulled my cock out and lined it up with her entrance. I wrapped one hand around her throat, restricting her breath, and then slammed inside her.

Avery's eyes shot open and remained wide. Her face was already turning red as she struggled for breath, each thrust of my cock making it more difficult.

I fucked her hard enough to bruise her—sore was the goal.

Her cheeks started turning purple, but her cunt was squeezing me.

"I'm almost there, baby," I assured her, refusing to let her breathe. "Squeeze my cock with that little cunt." Her walls clenched. "It feels so goddamn good when you do that," I groaned.

I released her throat and grabbed her hips. My thighs tightened, the edges of my vision blurring as I pounded into her with short, brutal strokes, filling her with my cum. I stared down at her the whole time, watching my little kitty take me, watching her break all over again as she came on my cock at the end of my own orgasm.

22
Avery

Rowen carefully cleaned me up with a warm cloth, like he was afraid too much pressure might break me.

A huge contrast from what he'd literally just put me through. I was surprised I was still in one piece after the way he'd fucked me.

And I was still cuffed to the bed, helpless.

He got the sheets out from under me and put new ones on before bringing the food to the bed, sitting down next to me with the fork in his hand.

"I can feed myself."

"I know," he said gently, patient but firm, pushing the fork to my lips anyway. "Eat, baby. Let me take care of you. You've been through a lot today."

I wonder whose fault that was.

The sudden softness gave me whiplash. He acted as though he hadn't cuffed me to the bed for hours and then fucked me raw after making me promise to never leave.

"I'm not hungry," I said quickly, pressing my lips together so he couldn't shove the fork between them.

He didn't look convinced. The fork remained pointed at me, a small bite of chicken on the end.

I couldn't eat. My thighs were sore. My pussy ached. My throat felt shredded from all the crying and screaming.

"Let me go."

"No." My stepbrother shook his head and sighed. "I can't do that, not when you tried to leave without telling me. I thought we trusted each other. What was that? Why would you sneak out in secret?"

Tears stung my eyes, and I tried swallowing the lump in my throat. "I wasn't *leaving* leaving. I told you I wanted to see my mom. You kept saying no, and I didn't want to fight anymore, so I figured I'd be gone for a day or two and then come back."

"You should've told me," he said, his broken heart on his sleeve. "How can I trust you?"

"How can I trust *you*?" I clapped back, pulling at my wrists for emphasis. "People don't tie their partners up when they try to leave the house."

His expression didn't change. He put the food down—thank goodness, because my appetite was nonexistent—and leaned in until our noses touched.

It was odd, the way he looked at me, like he still hadn't figured out how to handle me, how to hold me gently while loving me hard.

"I'm sorry, Av," he said after a while. "I lost it when I thought you were leaving me. I can't lose you. I won't. I'd rather keep you chained to the bed for eternity than go a day without you in it."

My breath hitched at his heavy confession, my heart trying to decide whether it was beating fast out of fear or something else, something deeper, darker.

Rowen's obsession, his need to *have* me, control me, scratched a need I didn't know existed. He'd changed my entire being, slowly breaking me down until my pieces fit his perfectly with his. Then, he'd absorbed me, until there was no me and no him.

Only us.

"I just want to see my mom, see if she's changed, if she can accept us," I told him, hoping he'd understand it wasn't me wanting to get away from him.

Several beats of silence followed, and we just sat there, staring at each other, both stubborn, refusing to give in.

Sighing, Rowen backed away from me and rubbed his hand over his face before looking out the large glass doors to our bedroom balcony. Then, he turned to look at me. "What if I give you something else?"

"I don't wan—"

"I'll get your mom here," he cut in. "I'll fly her out so she can stay for a night or two."

My chest swelled with happiness, seeing how willing he was to keep me happy, to give me what I needed and wanted.

I nodded at him, a lump forming in my throat. "Thank you."

He looked relieved and leaned in to kiss me. "I'll call her in the morning." The next kiss was hard and punishing, a lesson, then softened until his kisses turned into feather-like grazes. "I know I'm not doing this the way I should, but I'm trying. For you." His voice was rougher, like he was holding back. "I love you so fucking much."

There they were again, those words.

No hesitation, just his truth.

I didn't trust myself to speak, though, not when I was torn between distancing myself and crawling back into his arms.

He watched me, waiting, seeming patient, but I knew him better than that. We both knew his control was tight around me, and he could snap at any moment, demand whatever he wanted, even if I was unwilling.

Still, my heart skipped a beat, wanting to force those words from my lips, but my brain hadn't caught up yet. I'd missed every opportunity to say them back, to let him know I felt the same way, but could I really say it now?

Cuffed to his bed, wrists sore. High on being edged, thighs slick with our mess.

My brain was pointing out the red flags, telling me Rowen was losing it, that he was dangerous.

You should probably get the hell out of here the moment you can.

It was true. Rowen was unhinged, unbalanced, and obsessive, but I found myself craving it rather than being repulsed.

His love looked nothing like what it should. It was dark and relentless, and it came with a pleasure so intense, it felt like a punishment. That didn't mean he was dangerous. He wasn't a threat to me. He didn't cuff me to the bed to hurt me. He just couldn't stand the thought of losing me.

I opened my mouth then closed it, since I still couldn't say it.

It wasn't that I didn't feel something. It was that I felt *too much*, and I wasn't ready to open that dam. Not like this.

"Can you let me out of these?" I asked quietly, feeling guilty for not saying what he needed to hear.

His eyebrows furrowed, eyes boring holes into me, digging. His jaw ticked once, and then he blinked, the look of yearning fading into remorse—softened with a small smile.

"Let me feed you first."

I thought about saying no—I should have—but instead, I nodded and opened my mouth when the fork full of food came near my mouth, letting him feed me.

Showing him what I couldn't tell him.

I trust you.

***

I blinked awake and turned over to find the bed empty.

My wrists ached faintly, just enough to remind me what he'd done.

What I'd let him do.

Rowen fed me bite after bite, carefully cutting everything, watching me chew like I was fragile, and he had to be ready to catch me.

Then, he uncuffed me, only to hold me all night. Even when I shifted in my sleep, he was always there, repositioning himself to keep his arms wrapped around me. I should've felt caged, imprisoned, but I slept like a baby.

It was jarring, feeling so safe in the arms of someone who didn't know how to love without taking everything. Who was willing to do what it took to keep me, even if it meant going against my will. Someone who tied me up and still whispered his sweet love in my ears.

Moving slowly, my body aching with every step, I made my way downstairs.

He wasn't in the living room or the kitchen, but once I made it across the house, I could hear his voice, low and hushed.

His office door was cracked just enough to let me see him pacing with his phone to his ear.

"I don't need you to like me, Marissa. I get it. You hate me for what I did, what I took, but she wants to see you. Don't you just want her to be happy? She's your daughter, for fuck's sake. Just come visit her."

My stomach twisted. He was talking to my mom.

I should've walked away, but I was stuck to the floor, listening, my heart pounding in my ears.

"She's not a prisoner," he said, colder this time. "She's here with me because that's where she wants to be."

Well...

It was mostly true.

"Avery isn't a little girl who needs your permission. She's made her choice. Don't be stubborn about this. She *asked* for you to come visit. I can get the next flight out and have you here by the end of the day. Just let me know when you can show up for your daughter."

There was a pause, and I pressed my hand to the cool wall, letting it ground me.

Rowen was trying to play nice, trying his best to give me the one thing I'd asked for, no matter how much it hurt him.

"She loves you. She *wants* to see you," he said, quieter, like it broke him to say it. "So come see her or don't. But if you make her choose," his voice had dropped into something darker, rougher, "you will lose her."

I barely had time to pull away from his door when he ended the call. I rushed down the steps, but I wasn't fast enough.

Rowen cleared his throat just as my foot left the last step. I turned, my chest aching with deep emotion when his eyes met mine.

His mask dropped, releasing the tension and frustration he had been carrying. He softened in a way he only did for me.

"Morning, baby." His voice was deep and wrapped around me like a warm blanket, making my toes curl.

It was mesmerizing, the way he descended the stairs effortlessly and pulled me into his arms—something straight out of a fucking movie. He held me close, like he was starved for the physical contact.

His lips landed on my forehead, then my cheek, then my lips. The kiss stayed slow and steady, like he had all the time in the world to claim me, to remind me who I belonged to.

"I'm sorry I wasn't there when you woke up," he murmured against my skin. "Especially after last night." He pulled back just enough to search my face. "How do you feel this morning? Still sore?"

"A little," I admitted.

His lips spread with a wicked grin. "I spent the morning planning something to make up for it. I know it doesn't fix things, but I want you to know I'm trying to be better for you." He brushed my hair behind my ear, his thumb dragging along my jaw, making me shiver. "I made you breakfast. I'll feed you, and then we can take a long soak in the hot tub." He rubbed his thumb over my bottom lip. "And how does a full body massage sound? I won't even tie you up this time." Our lips were nearly touching. "Unless you ask me to."

Heat bloomed low in my belly. I was ashamed my body had forgotten his wrongdoings so quickly.

"You made breakfast?" I asked, trying to hide the effect he had on me, trying to remain casual.

His grin deepened. "Of course I did. It's my job to take care of you."

He led me to the dining room, his hand on my lower back. Dishes of eggs, potatoes, sausage crumbles, and cheese—for breakfast bowls—were on the table, alongside some cut fruit and mugs of coffee, mine looking the perfect shade of brown.

He knows me so well.

We mostly ate in silence, but it wasn't awkward or uncomfortable. Every so often, his foot would brush against mine. He even fed me small bites, watching me eat like it was mesmerizing.

When we finished, he took my hand and led me to the steaming hot tub outside.

Rowen removed his clothes and climbed in first then offered his hand.

I pulled the shirt over my head and dropped it to the floor. When I was about to take his hand, I hesitated—barely—but he caught it immediately.

"I won't push you," he said softly. "I know I came on strong yesterday, but I meant everything I said. I can't exist without you. I love you, Avery. I'll wait for you to catch up, however long you need, but I need you to know I love you more than anything. I always will."

He was so intentional with every word, like he knew exactly what I needed to hear.

I nodded slowly and let him help me into the water.

It was warm, perfect really, easing my sore muscles the moment I sank into the water. Rowen pulled me into his lap, and I leaned back against his chest, his hands sliding over my shoulders and down my arms.

"So, is she coming?"

Rowen froze for a moment then said, "I honestly don't know."

"You didn't have to threaten her."

"I didn't threaten her." He laughed. "I just told her to make her choice."

His hands moved to my back, massaging the tension away, then did the same for my thighs and hips.

I should've been mad at him, but I melted anyway. I knew this was him trying. In his own fucked up, controlling way—he *was* trying.

And I didn't want him to stop.

23
Rowen

I hated being away from her. Even though I worked from home, taking most of my meetings from my office, it felt too far. On especially long days, I loved finding her upstairs, waiting for me.

"What do you think you're doing?" she asked as I crawled onto the bed, immediately burying my face between her legs, cursing the clothes keeping us apart.

"Don't pretend you don't want it," I clapped back in a playful voice before nipping her inner thigh.

"Hey!" She swatted at me lightheartedly.

I looked up at her, her cheeks blushing immediately, almost like every dark, depraved thing I wanted to do to her flashed across my forehead for her reading entertainment.

Her eyebrow raised when I pulled on the waistband of her leggings, but I was the winner of our stare-off, and she lifted her hips enough for me to pull them down her legs. She was wearing red, see-through panties.

"Fuck, Av," I growled, looking back up at her. "Was someone *hoping* her stepbrother would fuck her?"

She refused to meet my eyes, embarrassed.

"You're so sexy. Body of a goddamn goddess." I kissed her thighs, then her stomach. I continued the path until I was taking off her shirt and kissing her neck and face, making her giggle. "I hope you didn't want to keep these panties."

"Wh—"

I tucked my fingers inside her underwear and tugged, my cock jerking as the rip of the fabric filled the room.

"Ro—"

I grabbed her face and pressed my lips to hers, silencing her protests.

"Mine, Av," I said, letting the possessive tone vibrate in my chest. "Do you understand that?"

She didn't respond at first, but then, she nodded.

"Spread your legs," I demanded as I kissed a path back down her body. "Hold them open, little kitty. I don't want anything getting in the way of my feast." I placed her hands on the backs of her thighs, showing her what I expected.

She squirmed when I kissed her mound, whimpering as thought I was already fucking her. Her eyes blew wide open when I slipped two fingers inside.

"Look at you," I breathed, spreading my digits as I fucked her slowly. "So fucking pretty. So fucking wet."

My thumb brushed over her clit, and she gasped, her hips jerking up. My cock throbbed at the sight, but this was *my* punishment. Tonight was purely about Avery getting off as many times as she needed, and I would go to bed without the luxury of fucking her.

"Row—"

I flattened my tongue against her clit and then sucked on it, listening to her broken moans fill the room. She kept herself pinned open for me with her hands, but her hips kept wiggling, trying to get away from me.

"Stay still," I growled.

I fucked her harder, my tongue flicking and circling her clit until her legs shook and her back arched off the bed.

She was coming undone, but I didn't let that stop me. If anything, I worked faster, and when she screamed my name, I knew she was there.

Her cunt gushed all over my face, soaking the sheets under us as her walls clenched down on my fingers. Even then, I didn't stop. I licked every part of her, cleaning her up, kissing her thighs, memorizing the way she twitched under my touch.

"Please..."

Her cheeks were flushed as I met her eyes.

"Please, what?" I whispered, kissing the inside of her thighs, my fingers still buried deep inside her.

She just whimpered, but we both knew she wanted to beg for another one, so I slid a third finger inside her and curled them just right. Her entire body jerked as I worked steadily and gently until she was gushing again, her mouth open on a silent cry as her fingers dug into her thighs.

Once her pussy relaxed around my hand, I slowed my pace but never fully stopped. I brushed my thumb over her clit, kissed it, and then toyed with it some more.

"Please...Rowen, I can't—"

"You can," I told her, keeping my voice low and commanding. "You will."

Her face twisted, body tight and shaking as I picked up speed, pulling another orgasm out of her, though this one lacked the previous splashing. She looked tormented and euphoric all at once, moaning my name half-heartedly with her eyes closed, gasping for breath.

"Fuck, you're so perfect," I panted as I withdrew my fingers to lick them clean, moaning as I ate the last remaining bit of her juices.

She let go of her thighs, but she didn't move much more than that, half-asleep already. Her body was shuddering as small rivers of tears ran down her temples.

I pressed my lips to her stomach then her chest, planting a firm kiss on her lips before sliding my tongue inside her mouth. She mewled, trying to kiss me back, but she was nearly limp.

When I pulled back, a smile spread on my face. She was a beautiful sight, all radiant and ruined, tired from her surrender.

She finally blinked up at me, but her eyes were glazed. Her lips even parted like she was going to say something, but no sound came out.

I held her tight, pressing kisses to her forehead as her breathing steadied and slowed until she was asleep. Reluctantly, I pulled away, slipping out of bed to grab a warm cloth. I cleaned her up slowly, gently, wiping her thighs and stomach, taking extra care not to wake her.

She stirred slightly when I pulled the waterproof sheets out from under her and replaced them with clean ones. By the time I tucked her in, she was out cold again.

After tossing the soaked sheets into the washer, I returned to our bedroom and sat on the edge of the bed, watching her sleep. My finger traced her face, the lines of her lips and her soft eyebrows. She looked so innocent, so small.

She deserved the fucking world and everything in it.

I wasn't the best at being soft and tender, but there would come a day when another little girl would be in this house.

Our daughter.

She'd watch the way I loved her mom, watch me spoil and worship her, protect her from everything dangerous in the world.

I would be the one to set the example of what love looked like, of what our little girl needed to search for when she grew up. I had to do better. I needed to show Avery I could love her the way she deserved, show her she was more than just my obsession, my perfect little fucktoy. She was my universe.

I reached down and tucked a strand of hair behind Avery's ear, smiling as she sighed in her sleep.

I wasn't planning on telling her about the deep thoughts I was having, but I'd show her—every goddamn day. And one day, she'd look at me and see the man who was willing to do anything for her, see the man who was stepping up and giving her everything, not the monster who locked her away.

I lifted the covers and lowered my head to her stomach, pressing a soft kiss there.

One day.

Avery stirred, a tiny whimper slipping out.

So, I brushed my lips against her ear and whispered, "I've got you, baby."

24
Avery

"I have a few suggestions to make regarding your launch," he said to his client, smiling at me when I appeared in the doorway of his office.

"Can I come in?" I mouthed.

When he nodded, I stepped inside and walked over to him, being careful not to step in the camera's view, but that didn't mean I was above distracting Rowen. I stopped in front of his desk and pulled my shirt up.

Rowen's jaw ticked, his eyes darkening with every passing second.

The client said something back to him, but I wasn't paying much attention. Neither was Rowen.

"Hey, Kyle, can you give me just a moment?" He smiled at his client, but even I could see the way he was barely restraining himself, the way his neck muscles were tight, his nostrils flared with deep breaths. "I have something I need to take care of right quick before we keep going."

He clicked a couple of buttons and rose from his seat. My feet were cemented to the floor, eyes glued to him as he stalked around his desk, his gaze never leaving mine.

The way my body responded to him before his hands ever touched me was intense, heavy. I could already feel his fingers brush my skin, his lips against mine.

My pussy was clenching, anticipating his hands, his tongue, his cock, knowing, *needing* what only he could give me.

I'd forgiven but not forgotten his actions from the other day, but he made it easier with the way he'd been taking care of me, constantly giving me gifts and snacks and insisting on a massage every couple of hours. The way he worshiped my body, took his time making sure I was so warmed up by his gentle touches...I was begging for his roughness.

I knew he was sorry, knew he was trying to be better for me, even if it went against every instinct he had, even if it meant loving me a little more gently than he wanted.

"I am in a very important meeting, Ms. Wilcox," Rowen said with a playfully stern voice.

It sent shivers down my spine.

"I'm so sorry, *Mr. Thompson.*" I giggled. "I didn't mean to interrupt you." My teeth tugged at my bottom lip as I batted my eyes innocently. "I just couldn't stop thinking about you."

His eyes flashed with something deviant, and I swallowed hard.

"You need to be taught a lesson, kitten," he murmured, now close enough to me that I had to look up at him. "Don't you agree?"

When I opened my mouth, nothing came out, so I just nodded.

"Bend over," he ordered. "Hands on the desk."

I did as he asked, placing my palms on the edge of his desk, the position pushing my ass out. He groaned when I slowly swayed my hips to tease him.

He stood behind me, his hands finding their way to my hips. He forced my movements, making me grind my ass against his hard cock, so hard, I was surprised it wasn't tearing through his clothes.

"I'll spank you as a punishment," he stated plainly, and my cheeks instantly heated.

His fingers slipped below the waistband of my shorts, pulling them over my ass and down my legs, abandoning them at my knees.

"*Fuck.*" My heart raced at his reaction to me. "You're such a little slut, coming in here during my meeting, flashing me your perfect tits, and all while you weren't even wearing panties." He pressed one of his hands on my lower back. "You definitely earned this."

Smack!

He didn't hit me that hard, but he'd put enough power behind it to make it sting. I gasped and tried to stand, but he kept his hand on my back, holding me steady.

My pussy confused the pain for pleasure, though, and I could already feel my heartbeat in my clit. My body was desperate for him already, and all he'd done was spank my ass like I was a naughty student who'd interrupted my professor's important meeting.

"One isn't enough for you," he said in a deep voice.

Smack!

"Oh my God..."

"He isn't going to help you," Rowen responded. "One more."

Smack!

The last one hurt the worst, and I had to close my eyes and grit my teeth for a few seconds.

"Thank me for your punishment, Ms. Wilcox."

"Thank you, Sir," I said, keeping in character with our little role play.

"You're excused."

I turned around, scoffing. "What?"

Rowen smirked at my shock.

"Did you really think I was going to reward such bad behavior?" He wrapped his arms around me and kissed my forehead. "You can go wait for me to finish my meeting, and then I will think about giving that needy little pussy some relief."

My thighs rubbed together, and I quickly pulled my shorts up to hide them. "I thought..."

Rowen sighed, looking like he wanted to indulge but was holding himself back. "I would, but I really do need to finish this meeting. I already postponed him twice to spend time with you." He leaned down and pressed his lips to mine. "And I don't want to rush worshipping your body, Av. I want to take my time to break you down until you can't take anymore."

Oh. Well, in that case...

"I'll wait for you downstairs," I said with a flirty smile.

He was already back to his meeting by the time I left his office.

My stomach growled when I reached the bottom of the stairs, and I instantly headed for the kitchen. Rowen was usually cooking dinner at this time. My body—more importantly, my belly—had the schedule down perfectly, but the meeting was lasting longer than he'd expected.

You can cook for yourself, you know...

I never had to, though. Rowen always insisted on cooking my meals. Even on the day he was gone, he'd left prepped meals in the fridge that just needed to be heated up.

Why waste perfectly good food? Rowen was a five-star chef as far as I was concerned, whereas my food was much less desirable.

I was spoiled, but I wasn't going to complain about being taken care of.

It was my turn to return the favor. He worked so hard and still found time to cook and pamper me. I wanted him to come down and find me in the kitchen, making him something special. Then, he'd *have* to finish what we started in his office.

I looked through the fridge, peering at every shelf and in every drawer, cataloging the ingredients we had. Then, I opened the cabinets, searching for something that could pair with the chicken I had found.

The spice cabinet was next, and I moved around the various jars and bottles to get a good look at what was there.

That was when I noticed the box on the top shelf, hidden just well enough behind some jars that I wouldn't have noticed it had I not been thoroughly searching.

I dragged a chair over and used it to reach the top shelf, pulling the box down to the counter. When I lifted the lid, I saw a leather journal, a glass bottle with a label that read 'Fertility Supplements', and stacks of pill packs.

My birth control.

But why did he have fertility supplements?

I grabbed the journal and opened it up, my eyes widening, stomach dropping, as I read the entries.

'June 1. Hid powder inside her fruit parfait. Had sex before bed. Came inside her.'

'June 2. Hid powder inside her chicken tacos. Had sex in the office. Came inside her.'

'June 3. Hid powder inside her smoothie. Had sex on the porch and in the shower. Came inside her both times.'

It was a log, complete with dates and meals and sex and...

He was hiding the fertility powder in my food? Why was he logging every time he came inside me? Why did he have so many birth control packs?

"Oh my God..."

Suddenly, I couldn't breathe. My heartbeat pounded in my ears. Tears clouded my vision.

Was he...

I sobbed into my hand.

Was he trying *to get me pregnant?*

"No, no, no..."

I tried to assure myself he wouldn't do that, that Rowen wasn't capable of deception like that, but I couldn't be sure. My stepbrother was more than intent on making sure we stayed together, lived our perfect life without interruption.

If he was afraid of me leaving, wouldn't trying to get me pregnant solve the problem? Keep me tied to him? Make it harder for me to escape?

No.

Rowen wouldn't...

But the box. Everything inside. The logbook.

I swallowed my emotions down and put everything back into the box, sticking it in the cabinet and sliding everything in front of it again, my mind still racing.

His footsteps sounded, and I quickly put the chair back and closed the cabinet, wiping the tears from my eyes, hoping he wouldn't notice, wouldn't question.

"Hey, kitten," he dragged when he got to the kitchen, his eyes scanning me like an assessment. "You okay?"

I forced a smile and nodded. "Yeah. I was just trying to figure out what to cook for dinner. I wanted to surprise you."

He chuckled, and even though I was a little terrified of the man in front of me, his smile still warmed my belly. "You don't have to cook for me. I like feeding you."

"I know." I fumbled with my hands nervously. "You just do everything, and I want to be useful."

He closed the distance between us and pulled me to him, looking down at me like I was the meal. "You are more than useful, baby, and besides, I enjoy taking care of you."

I stayed still as he leaned down and kissed me, and my body reacted instantly, my lips moving against his, my throat forcing me to moan at his touch.

His eyes were full of hunger when he pulled away, and I knew it wasn't for dinner.

"Can we cook together?" I suggested with a smile, hoping he'd take the bait.

At first, he didn't respond, and I was sure he saw through me, but then, he smiled and nodded.

"Sure." He let me go, and I backed up, trying to keep it together, wondering if he could feel the way the air between us had changed.

I didn't think so, because he turned and started pulling stuff out of the fridge as he talked about the meal he'd planned to make.

I wasn't really listening, just wondering how long I could bide my time. I had to wait until the perfect moment to bring it up, to demand the truth once and for all.

25
Rowen

I spent the entire week pampering Avery, more so than usual, complete with a gift on the breakfast table every morning. I rescheduled many of my meetings so I could have extra time to give her massages, watch her favorite movies, and feed her snacks. She laughed when I offered to buy her a goddamn puppy.

Avery finally breached the conversation during lunch, saying I needed to move on if I wanted her to act normally. She said I was going overboard with my gestures, that it was a constant reminder of what had happened.

So, I promised to stop—right after I hand-fed her the filet I'd cooked and carried her up to our bedroom so she wouldn't have to walk.

I just wanted to spoil her.

"Can we try something new?" she asked when we got to the room, her voice smooth and sexy.

She had no idea I'd try anything for her. If Avery asked me to dive off a cliff to prove my love, I'd do so without even looking to see what awaited me at the bottom.

"I'll try anything for you," I said as I kissed her again, my mind already racing with what wildly erotic thing she might suggest. "What did you have in mind?"

She pushed me onto the bed then pointed at the headboard.

At the cuffs still hanging there.

A reminder to us both.

For her, a symbol of just how entangled we were, how obsessed I was, how willing I was to do whatever it took to keep our love alive.

For me, a representation of my momentary lapse of control, a warning of what the future might look like if Avery didn't feel loved and secure here with me.

"I just thought it might be nice if you showed me some trust for a change," she interrupted my thoughts. "I feel like I've given you plenty, but I wondered if you'd... You know what? It's stupid. Just forg—"

"I'll do it." I pulled her to straddle my lap. "Anything to prove how much you mean to me." I pressed my lips against her collarbone, listening to her breathing change. "I mean it, Av. You're everything to me, and I love you so fucking much. I'll spend every last one of my goddamn days proving it to you."

The corners of her lips curled up just slightly. "Okay."

She bit her lip nervously as she slid off my lap and gestured for me to get in position.

I sat with my back to the headboard and watched her straddle me again. I was totally enamored by her as she placed her fingers on my chest, tracing the inked lines—her brand, the symbols —like she was trying to memorize the picture they painted. Then, her hands moved down one of my arms to wrap around my wrist and bring it up to the cuff.

She buckled the strap then looked at me.

"Is it too tight?" she asked softly, her breath warm on my face.

I shook my head.

My heart was pounding hard enough to leave my chest as she did the same thing to my other wrist. I swallowed hard, resisting the urge to pull away. I remained still, trusting her.

The vulnerability tightening in my chest was unexpected, and I had to focus on breathing steadily. I was giving her something I'd never given anyone, here for the taking. She could do just about anything she wanted, and I was limited as to my options to stop her.

Avery grabbed something from the nightstand and showed it to me.

A blindfold.

Fuck, Av.

She was testing me, and she was right, but giving up control wasn't me; it didn't come easy. It didn't feel *right*.

But I was trying for her. For us.

If I could give up control for a moment, maybe she'd see past all my demons.

I stared at the black silk blindfold in her hand and nodded, breathing deeper than usual when she slid it over my face, stealing my view, making my heart rate spike.

She must've been terrified when I'd restrained her against her will. I was letting her do it willingly, and I was all stressed out for no reason.

Her hands cascaded down to my chest with a soft tickle of her fingers. Her lips grazed my neck, and I tilted toward her, chasing her. I was starving for her, needing her touch, her reassurance.

But she pulled away, and then her weight shifted off me.

"Avery?"

Nothing.

Every muscle in my body tightened. "Avery."

More silence.

"Avery." Frustration was rising in my tone.

Still nothing.

The air had shifted to cold and silent. All I could hear was my own breathing, my racing heartbeat. All I could feel was the panic curling in my lower stomach.

Was she leaving?

"I found your box," she said from somewhere in the room.

Fuck.

The box.

The pills. The logbook. The evidence of how far I'd gone to make her mine.

"What?" I was still in shock.

"The one in the kitchen, behind the spices." She didn't sound close, but she was calm—too calm. "I'm guessing I wasn't meant to find it."

My mouth went dry. "Avery, I don—"

"Is the birth control even real?"

I tugged at the cuffs, my chest tight, my throat aching. "Uncuff me, and we can talk about it. I promise, I'll explain every—"

"June 5. Scrambled eggs, bacon, and pancakes. Hid powder inside her pancakes. She ate both." There was a soft shuffle of paper, like she was turning the pages.

"Av, don't go through it alone. *Please*. Let me go and—"

"July 23. Had sex on the patio, in the living room, and in the bedroom. Came inside her all three times."

"Stop. Please st—"

"July 24. Her period is two days late. Will start watching for signs of...*pregnancy*."

She wasn't pregnant, and I knew that, thanks to the 'wellness check box' I told her I got her to make sure she was healthy and everything was okay. We drew her blood, sent it in, and a doctor emailed her all the details of her tests—sans pregnancy test, as I requested.

I bit the inside of my cheek, hating the way her voice broke, hating that *I* was causing her pain. Again.

If she'd just set me free. Let me tell her—

"When did you decide you were going to get me pregnant without telling me?" she asked quietly. "Before or after I started the fake birth control?"

"I swear to fucking God, Avery—"

"Before or after?" she stated again, venom in her voice.

My heart was pounding loudly in my ears, making it impossible to think. "I can explain everything. Just let me out," I rasped.

"No."

The same answer I'd given her when she asked me to release her.

Now I was the helpless one.

Not just restrained. Not just blindfolded.

But completely, *utterly* at Avery's mercy.

"You said you loved me," she continued, "but you kept this from me. You even fed me the bullshit lie that we could talk about it later, when we were *both* ready."

"I do love you," I snapped, hating how pathetic and desperate I sounded. "I love you so much, it fucks me up, okay? I can't bear the thought of losing you, Av." I yanked on the cuffs. "One day, you'll realize I'm too messed up and you'll want to leave. They always leave, Av. Everyone always abandons me. One day, you will too." My voice cracked. "I can't lose you."

"So you lie to me? You go behind my back and, what, *try* to get me pregnant?" Her voice was strained, like she was on the verge of tears. "It's one thing to try and get me pregnant, but it's a whole different game when you use fertility supplements to increase the chances. That's not love."

"Goddammit, Av—"

"All I can think about is what else you haven't told me."

"Nothing else, I swear." I pulled hard against the cuffs.

"Now you know how it feels to be tied up and unsure," she whispered. "To have no control over what happens next."

She was crying now. I could hear it in the way her voice shook. It cut through me, hurting more than anything I'd ever experienced.

"I'm hopelessly in love with you," I said, taking a deep breath and lying against the headboard. "I didn't tell you because I was afraid you'd say no, afraid you'd see how badly I wanted it and decide it was too much for you to handle. Once I started, I couldn't just tell you. I had to keep it secret because I knew you'd look at me like I was sick."

"You *are* sick," she choked out.

The silence that followed almost broke me.

"Avery," I begged. "Please. I need to see you. Let me fix this. I can fix it. *Let me fix it.*"

Her footsteps got closer. "The worst part is I still don't want to leave, even after knowing everything." Her sniffles were hard to listen to, each one a stab to the gut. "Maybe I'm the sick one." I felt the bed dip. "You make me feel like I'm losing myself, but I'm scared of who I am without you."

I licked my lips. "I love you even if you hate me. Even if you leave me cuffed to this bed forever. Even if you fucking hurt me. You're it for me, Avery. I have nothing if I don't have you." My throat tightened. "Please don't leave me. You have every piece of me, even the ones I swore I'd never let anyone see. So believe me when I say, I'll never let you go."

I felt her hand on my chest, right over her name. Her fingers trembled. Then, the blindfold came off.

When I opened my eyes, she was staring at me with eyes full of fury and heartbreak. Love was tangled in there too, fighting to break through.

We were both sick.

But we were sick for each other.

26
Avery

Rowen's eyes were bloodshot and wild, locked on mine.

I stared at his chest, at all the permanent reminders he'd always been mine. His breath stalled when I traced the letters of my name, let them fall to count the scars across his ribs.

Tiny goosebumps appeared on his skin, and I smiled to myself. By the time I met his gaze again, my heart was beating out of my chest.

I started to lean forward, my eyes flicking down to his lips. He anticipated the kiss, dragging his tongue across his bottom lip in preparation.

Just before we made contact, I stopped. "I'll never let you go either."

He looked up at me like I was the only thing keeping him alive. Cuffed. Vulnerable. He was shaking, his hands flexing like he was itching to touch me, hold me.

I should have felt triumph. Maybe peace.

Instead, I felt like I'd been cracked open.

"I can't think when I'm around you, though," I whispered, more to myself than to him. "Everything gets...foggy. Like I disappear, and all that's left is who you want me to be."

"Avery." He sat up, tugging at the cuffs again. "Don't do this."

"I shouldn't forgive you," I went on, my voice shaking, throat tightening. "You've been lying to me about different things from the very beginning. The maze at the club. Michael. Your obsession. Then this. You hid things from me." I tried swallowing my emotions down. "You don't know how to love, Rowen. All you do is devour like a—like a *monster.*"

"I *need* you," he growled, struggling harder now. "I've never needed anyone before..." He paused, looking down for a moment before his gaze shot back to mine so suddenly, I jumped. "You think I'm a monster? Fine. I'll be your goddamn monster." He was breathing hard. "But remember...you're the one who made me this way."

I stared him down, chest tight, tears forming again.

"I don't want to leave you," I admitted. "But a part of me does want you to suffer."

His eyes widened just enough for me to notice. "Avery..."

"It doesn't even make sense, does it?" I tilted my head. "That I want to punish you for what you did to me, yet I still want you? That I want to ruin you the way you ruined me?"

He shook his head. "No, baby. Please don't do any—"

"I *should* hate you," I cut in, shaking my head. "But I don't. I just want you broken." I paused for effect. "For me."

"Avery—*don't*."

But I was already moving. I backed off the bed quickly, grabbed my phone, and threw on a jacket. There was no plan, but I knew I couldn't stay.

Not like this.

Rowen was yanking furiously at the cuffs, and I knew there was a chance he would break away from the wooden headboard it was attached to if he tried hard enough.

I had to move fast.

"Avery!" his voice roared behind me as I reached our bedroom door. "You run from me, and I swear to fucking God, the second I catch you—"

I paused in the doorway and turned to look at him.

His chest was heaving, eyes feral. His arms stretched against the restraints, the veins bulging in his arms. "—I will fuck you so hard, you'll break for me."

I smiled—just a little.

Because that was what I really wanted.

I wanted it so bad it scared me.

But he'd have to earn that.

"Good," I said and slammed the door behind me.

As I ran down the stairs, I could still hear him screaming.

Let him.

Because when I came back—and I would, when I was ready—I wanted him starving for me.

Some unhinged, fucked up part of me needed to watch him fall apart, knowing, *hoping* he'd destroy me all over again.

I was a wreck by the time I reached the garage. Tears streamed down my face, and I was sobbing so hard, I couldn't take a full breath. I felt like if I stopped moving, my body might refuse to keep going.

Grabbing the keys was hard, sliding into the driver's seat and starting the car harder, but pulling out onto the driveway was nearly impossible. My heart and body begged me to turn around, begged me to go back upstairs and throw myself at the only man I'd ever wanted, ever loved.

But my brain told me to run, to get as far away from my stepbrother as I could, because that was the only way I could have a clear head to think about what I really wanted.

My mind raced as I drove down the dirt road.

What the fuck are you doing, Avery? What's the plan?

I knew the name of the nearest town, but I'd only been twice with Rowen—grocery shopping both times. The last time, we also stopped at the farmer's market, but when a man at a stall flirted with me while I looked at his vegetables, Rowen started getting the food delivered to the house, and we didn't leave again.

His jealousy and possessiveness knew no bounds. If he didn't like something, he would take care of it—his way. I was coming to realize there was only ever room for Rowen's way of things, and I had to accept that willingly or let him force me to submit to his will.

Because you know there's no escape.

I typed the town name into my phone and waited for the app to load the directions. We lived out in the middle of nowhere, and now that I was away from the Wi-Fi, my service was slow as fuck.

"Come on..." I muttered, shaking my phone, as if that was going to make it work faster.

I was so focused on my phone, I nearly ran off the gravel road. The car bounced as I turned the steering wheel to get it back on track. Instead of risking running off the road and having to walk back to the house with my tail tucked, I pulled over and put the car in park to focus on getting directions.

The route finally loaded, but then, the car made a funny noise and turned off.

Fuck. Fuck. FUCK!

I turned the key and pressed the gas pedal.

It didn't turn back on.

I popped the hood and got out to look at it—hoping all the knowledge of a mechanic might hit me in the next several seconds.

I huffed and covered my face as I leaned against the car.

This had to be a fucking joke.

All the energy from the day collected in my chest, creating unrelenting pressure, like a huge weight had been placed on it. I looked up into the sky and screamed, releasing everything, all the built-up emotion I'd been pushing down.

"Fuck you, Rowen Blake! Fuck you and your money. Fuck you and your stupid house. Fuck you and your giant dick! I hate you!"

I didn't, not really, but it still felt good to say.

Ding!

I grabbed my phone to see a text message.

Rowen: Did you really think getting away would be that easy, kitten?

Holy fucking shit...

I knew he'd get out, but I thought I'd be further away before he did.

Ding!

My stomach churned.

Rowen: The car won't work

Rowen: You're all alone

Rowen: And I'm coming for you

Rowen: RUN

Panic. Terror. Thrill.

Rowen was fucked up, but so was I. Even though I'd been trying to escape, a small part of me was glad he was still fighting for me, refusing to let me walk away from him, from us.

Come and get me, psycho.

After shoving my phone into my pocket, I took off into the trees, abandoning the car.

I ran as fast as I could, trying to get as far as I possibly could, hoping I was running *away* from the cabin, from Rowen. The adrenaline pumping through my veins gave me a little more endurance than usual, but it wasn't long before I was wheezing, needing a break.

I found a large tree and leaned against it, my hands on my knees, taking a few minutes to regain control of my breathing and convince my brain I wasn't actually in any danger.

Aren't you, though?

He was pissed, broken, *lost*, when I left him cuffed to the bed, screaming like crazy, making all sorts of threats.

He'd already cuffed me to the bed for wanting to see my mom, even when I promised to come back. I couldn't imagine what he was going to do this time.

That alone should have sounded the alarms in my head, but they were offline, their ability to function severed by the need I'd developed to be owned by my stepbrother from hell. To be chased and forced to submit. To be branded by him again and again.

Just thinking about him catching me had my puss—

I heard a distant yell, growing louder with each passing second.

No fucking way...

I ran in the other direction, but the noise kept getting louder. It was like for every one of my steps, Rowen was taking three or four times that, desperate to catch up with me.

"Get your ass out here, Av!"

My heart skipped beats. My legs locked up with fear. My head spun.

"Beg for my forgiveness, and I might show you a little mercy!"

I could hear his heavy steps snapping twigs and rustling the leaves. When I tried to look around, I ended up tripping over a rock, sending myself face-first to the ground.

I caught myself on my hands.

"Shit," I muttered as I looked at the cut across my palm, blood already welling up and dripping onto the ground.

"Gotcha."

27
Rowen

She fucking ran.

Cuffed me to the goddamn bed and left in my car.

And for what? Because I loved her too hard? Too much? Made her feel things she wasn't ready to admit?

She even said it herself.

"The worst part is I still don't want to leave, even after knowing everything."

She didn't *want* to leave. If anything, finding that box showed her just how deeply and madly I had fallen in love with her.

And she fucking liked it.

Avery claimed trying to get her pregnant without her consent was twisted and fucked up, but even she couldn't lie about the impact my obsession had on her. She liked the idea of my love being so vast for her, I'd literally do anything to make sure she was mine forever.

But she still ran.

Still abandoned me.

It hadn't taken me long to rip the cuffs from the headboard, but it was long enough for Avery to take off, leaving me to find alternative methods to bring her back.

Abandoning my car once I shut it off from my phone had been a smart move.

But then she ran into the forest.

With her phone.

After sending her those texts, already closing the distance between us, I watched her take off like a scared little animal into the woods from the tracking app I'd installed on her phone.

I'd drag her back kicking and screaming if that's what it took.

The little dot moved quickly in the other direction, but I was faster.

"You can't run from me, Av!" I yelled.

I continued the trek, closing in on her, stopping ever so often to yell threats, telling her what I was going to do once I got my hands on her.

And then, I spotted her.

Running.

Then tripping, her palms slapping the wet dirt.

"Stop running, baby!" I shouted, my voice wild and rough. "We both know how this ends!"

She twisted around and scrambled back on her ass. Her eyes locked on mine as I approached her, slow and deliberate, like a wolf finally cornering its prey.

She kicked at me. "Don't fucking touch me, you psycho!"

I lunged and caught her ankle as she tried to spin away. She shrieked, kicking harder, slipping to her stomach. Mud flew everywhere as she clawed at the dirt, but I still managed to flip her over. Her breath caught when she saw me.

Panic. Guilt. Lust.

It all flashed across her face.

"Where do you think you're going?" I growled. "You don't get to leave me, Avery. I will always track you down and drag you home where you belong."

And then, she hit me, a sharp, stinging slap across my cheek.

It didn't hurt, not physically. She hadn't struck me hard enough for that.

But my body still reacted, just not in the way she'd intended.

For a second, we just stared at each other—both of us breathing like we were drowning, jagged breaths that filled the forest.

Then, I laughed.

"Fuck, sis. I love the new foreplay," I murmured, dragging her body closer to me, inch by inch, across the muddy ground.

Her legs thrashed as she twisted, but I kept pulling her until she was beneath me, the weight of my body pinning her to the forest floor.

"Get off of me!" She bucked against me, trying to toss me off.

I gathered her wrists and pinned them above her head with one hand.

"You left me cuffed to the fucking bed, baby. You got in my car and drove away." I licked the single tear that fell from her eye, groaning at the salty taste of her fear. "You thought I'd just...what? Let you go? Let you leave me?"

She refused to look at me, her jaw trembling. "I wish you had." She was trying to sound strong and defiant, but the crack in her voice revealed her lie.

"Liar." I leaned in, my nose brushing her cheek. "You knew I'd find you. You *wanted* this."

She hissed, twisting under me again, but she didn't tell me I was wrong.

"That's what I thought," I said in a softer voice. "You want to submit to me, Av. You want me to *drag* you back. You like pretending you have a choice, but we both know the truth."

She shook her head. "You're wro—"

"I'm never wrong, Av," I cut her off. "You want me to make all your decisions, to keep you trapped in that perfect little life you've grown so fond of. Don't you love the way I take care of you? Make sure you have everything you could ever need? I poured every goddamn ounce of my heart into serving you, Av, to keep you happy."

She was crying, but I wasn't sorry for the things I'd done.

"Do you have any idea what I felt? Unable to hold you while you broke down?" My voice was fraying. "Watching helplessly as you walked out, leaving me as though I meant nothing to you?"

"You don't," she snapped.

But her body was arching up to meet mine, heat building where we touched. She was trembling, and not from fear, as my free hand stroked her bare thigh, reaching under her skirt.

I smiled smugly. "You can do better than that."

"I hate you."

I brushed my lips against her cheek, her jaw, her ear. "You *love* me, little sis."

"No. I fucking hate y—"

"You hate how much you *need* me," I whispered.

She whimpered as my hand made its way up from her waist, fondling her breast under her shirt, her lacy bra keeping me from her soft skin. When she turned her face toward me, armed with more arguments, I kissed her.

Hard.

She bit my tongue instead of kissing me back, hard enough that I tasted blood.

I growled, shoving my thigh between hers and grinding down until she gasped against my mouth.

"Strike two, little kitty."

"Go to hell," she spat.

"I'll drag you there with me."

Tears spilled from the corners of her eyes, falling to the ground. They weren't tears of fear, though; they were tears of shame. Avery knew she wasn't supposed to want this. She just couldn't help herself.

I smoothed her hair back, watching as her eyes fluttered shut. "You are mine, Av. I own every perfect fucking inch of you."

Avery turned her head to the side, like she was trying to hide her face. She couldn't hide from me, though. My little stepsister got off on being claimed, even when she pretended to hate me for it.

Her body was relaxed, all the fight seemingly gone, so I loosened my grip on her wrists.

She used the opportunity to swing at me again, catching the underside of my jaw with her nails, dragging little scratches into my skin. She shoved at my chest as hard as she could, teeth bared, coming at me like a ferocious animal.

"You don't own me!" she screamed.

That was when the last tiny thread of restraint I'd been clinging to snapped.

"I do," I snarled, voice low and shaking. "And I'll prove it to you."

Before she could twist away from me, I caught her wrists and shoved them down hard above her head, making her cry out, trapping them there in one fist. My other hand slid down her curves, catching her thigh and yanking it up around my waist.

Her eyes widened. "Don't you dare—"

"Don't what?" I pressed my hips into hers so she could feel just how fucking hard she made me, how much I loved our games. "Don't show you what happens when you trick me? When you run?" My fingers dug into her thigh, making her mewl. "I'm going to punish you out here, and once I'm done, I'll drag your limp body back home, where we'll talk about whether you need to be cuffed to the bed for the foreseeable future or not."

Her breath caught, pupils blown. She thrashed harder, but it was too late. Her body had already melted against mine the way I knew it would. The way it always did.

"You don't get to leave me cuffed to the bed, steal my car, and run away like you don't need me," I hissed against her throat, nipping at the soft skin.

"I really do hate you," she said as tears spilled down the sides of her face.

But her body was still betraying her. Her hips bucked up, grinding against me.

She was whimpering and biting her bottom lip.

I was tired of her lies.

I shoved her soaked panties to the side, pulled my sweatpants down just enough to slip my cock out, and drove into her with a single thrust.

She screamed, the sound full of fury but also relief. Her back arched off the ground, her body wanting me deeper, admitting what her mouth wouldn't.

"Say it, Avery," I growled as I thrust into her hard enough to rock her under me. "Tell me you're mine."

"No," she gasped, trying to shake her head, but her eyes were rolling back.

So, I fucked her harder.

Every thrust was both a promise and a punishment.

She tried to keep quiet, tried to hold back, but her involuntary moans were loud and laced with shame.

I released her wrists, but this time, she didn't fight. Instead, her hands clawed at my shoulders, as though she was trying to pull me deeper, begging to be ruined.

"You don't get to run from this." I could feel her clenching around me already, so I slipped my hand between us, finding her clit, making her gasp. "You can't run from me, from what we are. I won't let you."

She screamed as I fucked her deeper, harder.

Avery's whole body shook, and her cunt spasmed around me. She sobbed my name, nails digging into the flesh of my back, coming so hard, she was gasping for breath.

Good.

I wanted her to drown in it. In *me*.

"I want to fuck your ass, Av," I groaned, slowing my pace but keeping each stroke hard and deep.

Her body was limp under me as she whispered, "*Please.*"

We had no lube, no prep, but I had to have every part of her, even if it meant hurting her.

I pulled out of her pussy, ripping her panties and skirt off as fast as I could, and used my fingers to spread her juices down, pressing a finger against her tight hole. She whimpered, but I kept pushing until my finger disappeared into her, distracting her by rubbing her clit. I didn't give her long to adjust before adding another finger, then another.

I spit onto her hole, watching as it combined with her arousal, only slightly lessening the friction.

"Row..." she said breathlessly, her eyes closed, lost to the world around her.

"It's gonna hurt, Av, but we both know you deserve it, don't we?"

She moaned.

"That's right. My little sadist will probably enjoy me forcing my way into her tight little asshole."

I stretched my fingers, and she cried out. Her eyes fluttered open, wide and full of tears, but she didn't look scared; she looked hungry.

"It hurts," she whimpered quietly.

I'll pity you later, little kitty. Now? You'll pay for your sins.

After withdrawing my digits from her ass, I spit on my hand, using it to lube my cock. It wasn't nearly enough for what I was about to do, but I couldn't let Avery leave these woods without a punishment. It had been far too long since I'd had her like this.

I pulled one of her legs up, resting it over my shoulder, spreading her, then pressed the tip of my cock against her tight hole. I forced it to stretch around me, listening to her groan, chuckling as her hands came up, as if she could stop me. She pushed against my chest, but I didn't budge. I moved my hips forward, groaning as she squeezed around me.

Inch by inch, I watched my entire length sink into her ass. What little lubrication I'd managed to gather barely eased the friction, but every bit of pain was worth it. She'd earned this punishment, but so had I.

Avery was whimpering, her hands still on my chest, shuddering under me.

"Look at you," I said in a low voice. "Shaking like a little slut, and I'm barely moving." I bottomed out in her ass, pausing to let us both adjust. "You wanted this. We both know it. So now, you're gonna take it, every fucking inch."

I withdrew just an inch or so then slammed back inside her, making her scream, raw and desperate.

"You're not in control anymore, Av. *I* am," I snarled, gripping her thighs hard enough to bruise.

I rammed into her again, and her back bowed as another cry ripped from her throat. Her body shook like it couldn't take any more.

"Tell me who you belong to, little sis," I growled at her, watching her face twist in pain, though her mouth spent half the time gasping and moaning.

She shook her head, eyes closed.

So, I fucked her harder, deeper, all while pressing my fingers against her clit, blurring the line of pleasure and pain. She was helpless as I used her exactly how she needed to be used.

I let go of her leg and leaned over her—a new angle. "*Mine*."

28
Avery

It was unlike any pain I'd ever felt before.

But he didn't care.

Rowen fucked my ass anyway, making me scream, *relishing* the way I broke for him.

Just as I always did.

His brutality made me want to beg for mercy, but the way he pressed his thumb against my clit as he sank a few fingers inside my pussy had my toes curling.

I wasn't supposed to enjoy this.

I hated Rowen for everything he did.

Hated how my body clenched around him.

Hated the way my thighs shook with need.

Tears blurred my vision. My hands moved wildly, confused about what they were supposed to be doing. My body was stretched and filled to the point of tearing open. The burn of his cock in my ass was unbearable.

But I was wet anyway.

"Fucking say it," he snarled.

I choked on a sob, internally screaming at my body, begging it not to give my stepbrother the satisfaction of taking what he wanted.

But then, his fingers stopped strumming my clit, and the meld of pain and pleasure was overrun with agony.

My lips trembled. "I'm yours! I'm yours! Please! I'm yours!"

He shoved his fingers back inside, curling to hit the perfect fucking spot, conquering me once and for all.

As I squeezed his cock and fingers, screaming and crying, he whispered in my ear. "The only way you'll ever escape me is if you stab my fucking heart, Av. And even then, you'd better make sure it stops beating before you walk away, because there's not a damn thing that would keep me from you as long as I'm alive."

I could've begged for his forgiveness. I could've avoided this entire thing had I never left in the first place.

But I made him chase me.

He slammed into me one last time and held steady, leaving me full, stuffed, and overwhelmed.

And I broke.

I was tired of pretending I didn't want him, like I wasn't wired to crawl back to him, like I hadn't fallen madly in love with him.

"I'm sorry," I whispered, barely audible. I looked up to see his face soften—barely, just enough to show me he heard it.

Rowen eased himself out of me, but the burn remained, a cruel echo of what he did. My body trembled, muscles spent, lips parted with shallow gasps. I blinked away tears, trying to ignore the way pain pulsed between my legs with my heartbeat.

I couldn't move. Not yet. Maybe not for a while.

Crazy thing was, the ache in my heart was the worst part.

You tried to leave him.

Rowen didn't say anything at first; he just dropped his forehead to mine and breathed with me. His hands glided up my body gently, like he was afraid to break me. They shook—I felt it—like he couldn't believe what he'd just done, like he wasn't ready to let me go and see the aftermath.

He lay down next to me and grabbed my face, and then he kissed me, hard and desperate.

"I'd lose my goddamn mind if I lost you," he whispered between soft kisses across my face, his voice breaking, his thumbs brushing my face. "I'm sorry, baby. *Fuck*. I'm so sorry."

I didn't answer him, didn't trust my voice, wasn't sure I could speak right now without cracking.

"I just—" He kissed my jaw, then my throat, then my chest, moving between my legs again, but my body was too tired to react.

"You ran, Av. You fucking ran, and all I saw was red. I thought I lost you for good."

His mouth was nearly between my legs, his kisses still gentle, so careful, I almost sobbed from the contrast. One second, I was his filthy whore—his fucktoy—and the next, I was everything to him.

And, God help me, I enjoyed every bit of it.

"You belong to me," he said again. "You don't get to disappear. You don't get to leave me."

Tears slipped down my cheeks as he slipped two fingers inside me, and I gasped, the soreness between my legs overwhelming.

But he didn't stop.

He whispered sweet nothings, reminding me he loved me and would do anything for me while he stroked the spot that made my thighs shake.

I closed my eyes, savoring the gentle love.

Rowen ate me on the forest floor, physically and metaphorically. When he finished, he carried me back home, half-naked and completely ruined.

He was so gentle, holding me like I was the most precious thing he'd ever touched.

I wanted to hate him for what he'd done, for the way he'd fucked me up and made me need him. I wanted to scream at him, tear him apart, and tell him he had no right to love me this way, not after that.

But I couldn't help the way my heart beat faster when he squeezed me tightly. So, I buried my face in his neck, my body melting into him even though every inch of me throbbed, feeling safe despite the hurt.

He sat me down in the bathroom and started the bath then grabbed our softest towels and put them in the towel warmer he'd surprised me with weeks ago.

I tried to stand and get in the tub, but Rowen was there.

"Don't push yourself, baby," he said, getting in before me and helping me ease into the water.

When my ass landed on the bottom, I winced, and he flinched, like he felt it too.

He grabbed a soft cloth and dipped it in the water. He ran it down my arms, over my chest, between my thighs, careful everywhere I was raw. Every stroke was a word, an emotion he didn't know how to say. Every kiss he pressed to my temple was another broken apology.

"I don't know how to love you gently, Av," he whispered against my shoulder. "But I'm trying. For you, I'll try."

29
Rowen

I dried her off carefully before carrying her to the bed.

She didn't fight me anymore, but she'd stopped clinging to me like I was her lifeline. She was quiet, watching me with those soft brown eyes. Her thighs were still trembling, skin hot and pink from the bath, eyes puffy from crying.

I lay her down gently, wincing with her as her body met the mattress.

You did that.

After tucking the blanket around her, I sat beside her, pressing my forehead to her bare shoulder, grateful she didn't move away.

"You're the only thing that keeps me sane," I whispered, breathing her in. "If you ever leave me," my voice was still low, barely audible, "I'll still find you...even if it's years from now. Even if you try to forget me. Even if you find someone else."

I swallowed hard, watching the way she shifted under the blanket, her eyelashes fluttering. For a second, I thought she was going to pull away, tell me no, remind me that what I'd done to her wasn't love, it was madness, and she wanted nothing to do with it.

But she didn't.

She looked at me like she'd already forgiven me.

And it nearly broke me when she whispered, "I'm not going anywhere," just before her eyelids closed.

***

Avery was awake before me.

She slipped out of the bed—slow and quiet—but I didn't stop her, even if every muscle in my body wanted to grab her, cage her in. Instead, I remained still, my eyes closed, fists clenched in the sheets, waiting. I half expected her to run again; I wouldn't have blamed her.

I was already thinking about how to keep her here if she did.

She left the room, and I got up slowly, rubbing the sleep from my eyes. My chest was tight as I slipped on a pair of boxers and walked down to the kitchen, where I heard the cabinet open.

I found her standing at the counter, holding a bottle.

The fertility supplement powder.

She turned to face me.

"How long have you been putting this in my food?" Her voice was quiet, almost too calm.

I didn't flinch. It was time to give Avery the truth, expose every dark part of me, and let her decide if I was still worthy of her love.

"Since we moved in."

She blinked, her fingers curling around the bottle like she was going to throw it, but she didn't.

"Why?" Now her voice was shaking.

"Because I love you," I said simply. "I want to tie you to me. Forever."

Her breath hitched. "So you tried to get me pregnant."

It wasn't a question.

I nodded. "I did."

"Do you still want to get me pregnant?"

I nodded again and reached for her hand, but she stepped back.

"And the birth control? It's fake, right?"

I didn't answer; I didn't need to. She already knew.

The silence was deafening, but then she spoke. "I think I'm gonna be sick."

Her hand shot to her chest as she ran to the sink and heaved, but nothing came out. She turned with her finger pointed at me angrily. "I can't believe you—" She heaved again.

No words could comfort her, I knew that, so I didn't bother wasting them. Instead, I rubbed her back until she was finished and then led her to the bathroom, gesturing for her to sit on the toilet. I reached into a drawer and pulled out a pregnancy test from under some washcloths.

I'd had multiple stashed there—just in case.

I handed her one without a word and sat on the edge of the tub. I stared at the floor, listening to the soft sounds of her breathing, the tearing of plastic, the shuffle of her sitting on the toilet, all of it.

Neither of us moved. I wasn't sure I was even breathing at this point, and I didn't know how much time had passed.

"It's negative," she said after a while.

I looked up at her. She was holding the test with both hands. Her face was unreadable. Blank.

But her eyes.

They looked tired, almost a little discouraged.

Before I could ask her, she looked at me and said, "I know I shouldn't be disappointed. I just..."

I held out my arms, and she rushed over to me.

"There's nothing wrong with the way you feel," I said in a calm voice. I placed my hands on her hips and pulled her close, resting my face against her soft belly.

"Rowen?"

I looked up at her.

"I'm sorry I ran." Her eyes were glassy. A long silence stretched between us. "I keep thinking I'll stop wanting you," she whispered.

"That one day, I'll wake up, and all of this will feel wrong. But it never does. It just gets deeper. Scarier."

I nodded slowly. "That's love, baby."

She snorted. "That's not love. That's obsession."

"I don't see a difference."

"I love you."

For a second, I wasn't sure I'd heard her right, that I'd imagined the thing I wanted more than anything in the world, but then she said it again.

"Rowen, I love you. I do." She was crying. "I am hopelessly, madly in love with you, and I can't stop."

I sank to the floor and pulled her into my lap, wrapping my arms around her, never wanting to let her go.

"Fuck, Av." My eyes stung with tears. "I love you so fucking much."

I grabbed her face, kissing her with everything I had, holding nothing back, giving her all of me, promising to be better for her, for us, for our future.

"You tracked me down in the woods like a psycho," she whispered, but her words weren't laced with shame or regret. They were almost playful, curious.

I chuckled. "And you liked it."

"Maybe I did." Her voice was trembling again.

I brushed her lips with mine. "Nothing about us is right, baby, but fuck, is it the rightest thing I've ever felt."

She smiled softly and bit her lip. I rubbed my thumb along her cheek.

"I love you, Rowen Blake Thompson."

I fucking melted.

Epilogue 1
Avery
One Year Later

No more fake pills. No more hidden supplements. No more secrets.

Rowen had been reluctant but understanding when I told him I didn't want the fertility vitamins anymore. It made me feel like I had a choice—even if some part of me wanted the same ending he did. That was probably why I didn't pursue getting real birth control pills, but Rowen didn't bring it up either.

After he tossed everything into the trash outside, he said, "*We'll just be careful,*" and kissed me like it didn't kill him to say those words.

We weren't *that* careful, though. Not really.

We did try—kind of. We used condoms when we remembered, and I had a rough idea of my cycle's fertile window. During those times, we tried a little harder to be careful, but most of the time...we just didn't. Sometimes, he even begged to come inside me, and I didn't say no.

And still, month after month, nothing.

Every time I got my period, every time I saw the blood, I told myself I was relieved. It was a good thing I wasn't pregnant.

But I always cried in the shower afterward, claiming it was the hot water that made my face red and splotchy.

Rowen had me spread out on the bed, my arms cuffed to the headboard, my legs tied in what he referred to as a 'Futumomo'. It was the same way he'd tied me up before I let him carve his initials into my skin so many months before, the night we were caught together, the last time either of us had seen our parents.

My mom never responded to my texts, never called or texted Rowen to tell him to get her a way to our house. If she didn't want to be a part of it, so be it. Rowen was more than enough for me.

He'd been learning not to suffocate me with his love. I'd even been to the store in town a couple of times on my own, though I knew he was watching my location from his phone like a hawk.

I didn't hate it, though, and sometimes, the car 'broke down' on my way home and I'd text him to come find me before taking off into the trees.

"What are you thinking about?" he asked, finishing the tie on my right thigh. "You look a million miles away, baby."

I wiggled, testing his restraints. Secure.

"Nothing, really," I said with a small smile. "Just how much things have changed, how good they are now."

He smiled back, but his eyes were dark, and the curve of his lips looked more sinister than sweet. "There is one thing that hasn't changed, though, baby."

My breath hitched as he lined his cock up with my entrance, both of us totally naked, our brands, his ink, on display for one another.

"My insatiable need to have you thoroughly wrecked every fucking day," he growled before slamming into me with one, steady thrust.

I didn't have time to catch my breath before he was thrusting slow and deep, holding my face to keep my eyes on his.

"That's it, baby. You take it so well. Look at you, all needy for your stepbrother's cock."

He kissed me softly as he fucked me, his thrusts rough and possessive. Rowen took every opportunity to remind me I was his, so sex was hardly ever 'love-making', but that was fine. I wanted him any way I could get him.

"Row—" My own moans cut me off as I tightened around his cock, coming for him.

"Goddamn, Av. Just look at how pretty you are when you moan for me. Fuck, you're so tight when you clench down on me." His thrusts slowed just a bit once my orgasm faded. "I'm going to come too fast like that."

I was confused when he pulled out and disappeared into our closet, but my cheeks burned when he returned with an anal plug, nipple clamps, and my favorite toy—the rose.

"I want you shaking and speaking in tongues before I even consider untying you tonight."

I swallowed, knowing he meant what he said. Rowen had taken me to new heights, pushing my body and training it to listen and respond to him.

I had no complaints.

He grabbed the lube from the nightstand drawer and covered the plug before dripping some onto my ass. After providing me the courtesy of a single finger as prep, he pressed the large plug against my tight ring, slowly stretching me.

"Fuck!" I cried as the burning sensation grew, the voices in my head telling me it was too much, to stop him before he hurt me.

"You can take it, Av," he murmured, kissing my inner thighs. "Breathe and relax for me. You're doing so good."

I listened to him; I couldn't help it. My breathing slowed and my body relaxed. He pushed the last of the plug in, but then the thing came to life inside me after a soft click.

A *vibrating* anal plug.

Jesus-fucking-Christ. This man was going to be the death of me.

"Rowen! Shit!" My entire body came to life as he clipped the nipple clamps on, the lingering sting growing every second, the jingle of the bells sounding as I shook. "Please. It's too much. It's way too—"

"Already too much?" He held up the rose toy. "Baby, I'm just getting started."

I saw the goddamn light of heaven's gates when he put the little sucking toy over my clit.

Words refused to leave my lips. The only language my brain knew in that moment was moans and gasps. Rowen chuckled, watching me struggle to get control of my own pleasure.

I failed.

Miserably.

My lips parted on a scream—his name—as electricity shot through my body and a familiar feeling built between my legs.

Fuck.

Everything was so much more intense when there was a vibrating plug in my ass and clamps on my sensitive nipples. It wasn't long before I was gushing onto my thighs, the bed, and probably all over him, but he *loved* it. He'd made it his goal to make me squirt whenever he could.

"There you go," he praised as I continued to come, each wave of pleasure pushing more of me onto the bed. "It's so fucking hot when you do that, Av. Do it again," he commanded.

And I did.

Again and again and again, until I had no more left.

But he wasn't finished.

He turned the rose toy off and pressed his hard cock against me.

"Now I'm ready to fill your slutty little cunt," he said as he inched forward, easily sliding into me with all the wetness I'd built up during his torture. "*Fuuuuck,*" he drew out as he moaned, a sound I'd never not find hot as hell.

Each thrust pressed against my ass, fucking both holes at once.

"Please, Rowen," I begged, still shaking from the multiple orgasms, already on the brink of another one thanks to the plug inside me.

"I can feel it too, Av. The plug." He kissed me, hard but quick. "It feels good, doesn't it? Being so full and overstimulated."

I shook my head, but I loved it, loved being at his mercy, loved being pushed over the edge every time he got his hands on me, loved begging him to stop, knowing I didn't really want him to.

I loved being *his*.

"Such a good slut for her, aren't you?" he whispered in my ear. "You definitely are. Taking my cock in your pussy while you have that plug in your ass." He bit my earlobe, making me gasp. "Tell me, Av. Tell me how good it feels."

I didn't have long to tell him; an orgasm was just around the corner. "It feels so good. So fucking good. I'm so full."

It hit me hard. My toes curled to the point of cramping, my eyes rolled back, my spine arched off the mattress. I couldn't hear anything except the ringing in my ears as stars exploded behind my eyes. My body was trembling as the orgasm ripped through me, wave after wave, what felt like a few tag-along orgasms at the end.

"Just like that," he murmured in my ear. "Break for me, kitten. I'll catch you. I hold you together. Let it all go."

His steady pace helped prolong everything, but I couldn't beg him to stop. I couldn't even open my eyes. I just laid there until his thrusts got rougher.

"I need to come inside you," he rasped like a desperate man. "Please, Av. Ask me to fill your little pussy full of my cum. I need it, baby."

He never did it without my permission; his hot cum inside me was the best feeling ever.

How could I tell this man no?

I managed to nod and mumble 'yes', and that was all he needed. Seconds later, he spilled into me as he groaned my name.

"I love you so much," he said, voice low in my ear. "You've ruined me."

But it was I who was ruined.

By the time it was over, I was boneless as he eased out of me.

Rowen cleaned us up and removed the waterproof mattress cover, and then he slowly untied my legs, massaging them back to life. Once he uncuffed my wrists, he laid down and pulled me to his body, spooning me.

One of his hands held me tightly while the other explored my sweaty skin, barely tickling me, but it felt good.

He kissed my shoulder, my neck, my ear, anything he could reach.

And then, he pulled back.

"Do you feel okay?" he asked.

I blinked, still under the haze of sex, dazed after all those orgasms. "Yeah," I said, dragging the word out. "Why?"

He flipped me onto my back, tilting his head as he looked down at me. His eyebrows twitched, eyes searching mine, like he was trying to figure out what to say.

"You've been tired lately. Um...moody, even. And your boobs are...different. Sensitive."

I blinked several times.

"What?" My brain couldn't figure out what he was trying to say.

He reached into his nightstand drawer, like he'd been prepared, and pulled out a blue wrapped stick.

A pregnancy test.

I stared at it then him.

"You're late," he said gently. "Almost a week."

I froze. I hadn't even realized. I'd grown so used to the disappointment, I just stopped keeping track.

He hadn't.

"Take it." He handed me the test. "Just to know."

He was nervous, and it was making me nervous.

I stood slowly and went to the bathroom.

Time stood still as I took the test out, peed on it, and laid it on the counter. I grabbed a piece of toilet paper and tossed it over the little screen with the loading bar. After washing my hands, I sat on the floor, staring at the corner where the test sat.

Several minutes passed before Rowen appeared at the bathroom door. "You okay?"

I swallowed and shook my head, tears forming, way too many emotions welling up inside me. He came to me immediately, pulling me to him, letting me sob into his chest.

He didn't ask about the test; he just held me until I stopped crying, then held my chin as he pushed the tear-soaked strands out of my face.

"Do you want me to look?"

I shook my head. I had to be the one to look.

My fingers trembled as I stood and reached for the test. After a deep breath, I looked at it, then at Rowen still sitting on the floor. I didn't say a word.

I didn't have to.

"You're pregnant," he said like he was relieved, rising to his feet.

I nodded, feeling like I was going to cry and burst at the same time, my brain in shock.

"You're—" He cut himself off, chest heaving, and ran a hand over his face. He reached for me like he couldn't bear to be apart for one more second and wrapped his arms around my waist. "You're carrying my baby, Av. *My* baby."

"I am," I whispered, unable to hold back my smile.

"Holy shit, Av. We're having a baby." He kissed the top of my head. "I love you so much. So, so fucking much."

This time, when I cried, it wasn't grief or confusion. It was deeper.

"I love you too, Rowen."

Epilogue 2
Rowen
Nine Months Later

I wasn't a good man. I ruined everything I touched. I broke the woman I loved again and again. I wasn't capable of anything soft without spending every ounce of my focus on it.

But there I was, holding the smallest, most fragile thing I'd ever touched.

Our daughter.

She was sleeping in my arms, a tiny, warm bundle against my chest, wrapped in a light pink blanket like a present. Her fingers twitched, eyelashes fluttering, the only sound in the room was Ginny's quiet breathing.

And her mother's.

Avery was out cold, needing sleep after the birth. She'd more than earned it.

She was a fucking champ. She didn't just give birth, she conquered the whole damn thing. I'd never seen anything more brutal, more beautiful, than her face as she screamed through hours of labor, refusing to let go of my hand. I still had nail marks from the way she'd held on to me, voice hoarse as she screamed.

I wasn't sure how she did it, but she did, and when our little girl screeched for the first time, Avery cried tears of joy.

I didn't know I was capable of loving her more, but sitting in the chair, holding the little life we'd brought into the world together, watching her sleep...I was falling for her all over again.

She looked so peaceful.

Damp strands of hair stuck to her temple, her lips slightly parted. Her arms were still cradled the way they were when she'd fallen asleep with Ginny in her arms.

My eyes fell to the ring on her finger, the one I'd picked out for her after we found out she was pregnant. It wasn't *because* she was pregnant, but I wanted—needed—them both to have my last name.

Avery insisted on a courthouse wedding. We had no one to invite anyway.

She wore a short, white sundress that made her pregnant belly look so cute, and I wore my leather jacket. She'd never been more beautiful than that day, but she looked angelic now.

I had the urge to kiss every inch of her skin, to whisper how fucking proud I was over and over, to tell her I loved her more than anything, more than life, more than myself.

Ginny squirmed in my arms, and I watched her eyelids blink open. She had blue eyes, but the nurses told us they'd most likely change as she got older.

"I hope you get your mother's beautiful brown eyes," I told my daughter, brushing a finger over her soft cheek, her fingers, in awe of how tiny she was. How *beautiful* she was. "I'll never let anything happen to you or your mother. Ever," I promised.

We were meant to be.

Avery. Me. Ginny.

I'd chased her down, hurt her, and fucked her until she forgot how to walk, until her body learned to crave mine the same way mine did hers. I lied to her, obsessed over her, even slipped supplements into her food and bought her fake birth control just to make her stay with me.

And she did for some reason.

Not because I forced her.

She stayed because she *loved* me.

I didn't understand why, but I wasn't going to take it for granted.

I looked back down at Ginny, chest tight, like I couldn't breathe.

"You weren't an accident. You weren't a mistake," I told her, her eyes unfocused and cloudy but looking up at me, nonetheless. "You were always the plan, from the very beginning."

She made a small, sleepy sound like she approved, and I couldn't help but smile.

I looked back at her mother, still managing to look heavenly despite everything she'd been through in the last sixteen hours.

I adjusted Ginny in my arms and leaned back in the chair, letting my emotions settle into me.

"Hey..." Avery's sleepy voice broke through the silence.

Her brown eyes were exhausted but shining. She smiled, slow and lazy, like the world was perfect.

Mine sure was.

She looked at our daughter then back at me.

"I love you so much...*husband*," she breathed, a tear rolling down her cheek.

I got up, put the baby back in her arms, and kissed her softly.

"I love you too, my beautiful *wife*," I whispered back. "More than you fucking know."

And I meant it, with every twisted, fucked-up inch of my soul.

The sound of pots and pans clanging met my ears before I even stepped out of my office, and I found myself wondering what chaos I was going to find in the kitchen. I knew—we both knew—no matter how many times she read that recipe or watched someone explain how to do it, she'd present something god-awful on the plate. I'd tried many times to teach her, but I was convinced my wife would burn water at this point.

It didn't stop her from trying, though, and with Ginny coming home, it gave Avery even more reason to make something special.

Ginny was every bit like her mother—stubborn and passionate. She'd inherited my looks but was blessed with her mother's deep brown eyes. I never thought I could love something so much, but ever since they placed her in my hands, I'd vowed to protect her with my life, just as I had her mother's.

When she'd gone off to college, nearly four hours from the cabin, from her mother and me, I thought I was going to have a heart attack. I'd tried to move with her, but Avery didn't want to give up the home we'd made, so I settled for buying a small apartment near Ginny's school. We visited often, staying some weekends, even though Ginny assured us she was fine and didn't need our constant check-ins.

A loud bang from the kitchen brought me out of my thoughts, and I moved carefully, avoiding the creaks on the floor, making my way to my wife.

Avery moved gracefully around the kitchen, though she looked lost, cursing under her breath. I bit my lip to avoid chuckling, not wanting to signal my presence just yet.

She stared at a recipe from a cookbook cracked open on the counter, then went to the fridge, only to come back muttering as she scanned the pages again.

Even the mundane sight of her attempting to run the kitchen had my heart thumping. Avery was more breathtaking than the day we met, and every day, I found myself falling more in love with her.

She jumped when she turned, spilling a little of the flour from the measuring cup in her hand, and saw me leaning against the wall. "Fuck! Rowen! How long have you been standing there?" She frowned and swiped at the white powder on her flowery apron.

I smiled at her, and her expression softened as she shook her head and rolled her eyes. "I was admiring the view, kitten."

One of her eyebrows hitched up. "The view?" She gestured to herself, pointing at the hair sticking out of her bun, the sweat on her brow, the flour covering her front, and the bunny slippers on her feet. "Not much to look at here, but I still appreciate the compliment."

I closed the distance between us quickly, before she could turn and run. I grabbed the measuring cup from her hand and set it on the counter before dipping her to the floor, making her giggle.

"Mrs. Thompson," I said in a serious voice once I had her upright again. "You must understand something about me." I pushed some loose hair behind her ear, savoring the way her cheeks turned pink even after all these years. "I don't care if you wear a trash bag dress and sandwich bag shoes. I will *always* find the sight of you absolutely delicious."

I nuzzled her neck, breathing in her sweet smell before nipping, licking, and biting at her throat until she was moaning quietly, limp in my arms. Only then did I trail a path over her jaw until our lips met and kiss her with everything I had. I groaned when her tongue pressed past my lips, seeking mine. I was hungry for her.

Fuck dinner. I'll eat you instead, little kitty.

She was breathing hard when I finally pulled away, cheeks redder than a tomato.

"You've never looked more beautiful than today, baby," I promised her, keeping my arms around her waist, wanting her close to me.

"Rowen..." She licked her lips, eyes darkening with desire, and I could practically hear her pulse race.

"If Ginny wasn't going to be here any minute, I'd ravish you on the counter as an appetizer." I kissed her nose.

"Uh..." Avery gave me a nervous smile. "About that..." She patted my chest with her hand. "She's outside in the hot tub."

I released my wife and walked over to the sliding doors leading to the deck. "Avery."

"Yes?" I could hear the amusement in her voice, and it only irked me further.

"There's a boy in the hot tub with Ginny."

"His name's Henry."

Excuse me?

"Who the fuck is Henry, and why is he all googly eyes towards my baby?"

Avery laughed, and I didn't understand why she wasn't upset. "Ginny said she was bringing him home to meet us."

"I don't remember her saying anything about a...*boy*." I rolled my eyes and glared out the window at the guy sitting *way too close* to my daughter.

Avery came to stand by me, wrapping her arms around my waist and leaning her chin on my back. "That's because you told her she wasn't old enough to date and tried to pretend she was kidding even though she told you she was serious."

"You should've told me when they got here," I grumbled.

She shrugged, and my body instantly missed her warmth when she pulled away. "You said your meeting was important. I figured this could wait until you were finished. They aren't going anywhere anytime soon."

I turned to look at her, eyes wide. "But she brought home a *boy*, Av. That's an emergency. That's 'break down my door and slam my laptop closed' level emergency." I rubbed a hand over my face. "How am I supposed to scare him off now that he's all cozy in our hot tub?"

She laughed, amused by my predicament. "I'm sure you'll think of something."

"I have to get out there right now." I turned and walked out onto the deck.

Ginny turned, noticing me first. "Hey, Dad. Mom said you were... What are you doing?"

I got into the hot tub, clothes and all, and sat myself between Ginny and...*Henry*.

"Dad!"

"How old are you?" I stared daggers into the shirtless, tattooed boy sitting across from me.

"Twenty-one, sir." He smiled and stuck his hand out. "I'm Henry. Ginny's told me so much about—"

I turned to my daughter, who glared at me. "He's too old for you."

"I'm twenty-one in two weeks. We're pretty much the same age." She held my stare, daring me to say more.

Curse that stubborn Wilcox attitude she got from her mother.

I turned back to my enemy. "What are you studying?"

"Forensic science."

"What are your plans with my daughter?"

"Dad..." Ginny said warningly. "Chill out with the questions, okay? You're not an interrogator."

I narrowed my eyes anyway, and Henry nodded.

"I really like her, sir. I'd like to keep getting to know her, but she insisted that I meet you guys before we made anything official." Henry looked at my daughter, and it was clear he was smitten with the way his eyes softened as his grin grew.

I don't like it one bit...

I looked at Ginny with a smug smile of my own. "What happens if I say I don't like him?"

She snorted. "Mom likes him." She shrugged.

"You're too much like your mother." I rolled my eyes, but I knew I was defeated.

Ginny was in love. She might not have even realized it, but I could see it. The way they looked at each other made that clear.

It wasn't too late to scare him off, but I'd have to be sneakier about it, since Ginny's heart was involved. I'd be watching the boy like a hawk.

I looked at...*Henry*. "I'll be watching you very closely."

"Fair. I'd expect nothing less. I promise, I won't hurt Ginny. You have my word." He stuck his hand back out, and this time, I took it.

It was hard not to like his answers, but that didn't stop me from squeezing his hand just a little more than necessary to remind him I was a threat.

"I should help your mother cook dinner before she burns the house down," I said as I crawled out of the hot tub.

I took the stairs to our bedroom to dry off and change, and by the time I made it downstairs, Avery was cursing as the smoke alarm went off.

"What's going on?" I hollered over the beeping.

Avery opened the oven door, and even more smoke spilled out.

"Don't touch that. I'll get it." I took over, not wanting her to hurt herself, and removed the questionable item from the oven.

Avery opened the door as I grabbed a towel and fanned smoke away from the alarm. When it didn't stop, I grabbed a chair and removed the smoke alarm from the ceiling, ending the horrible noise.

"I'm so sorry," Avery said, laughing so hard, she was crying. "I thought I set the oven to 350, but—"

"350?" I snorted, looking over to where the bright numbers read '550.' "Baby, we need to get you some serious help. Gordon Ramsay would have a field day with you."

She giggled harder, doubling over as I neared her. "I wanted a nice dinner for us. I watched the video twelve times, Ro. *Twelve.* I was ready for this one."

I pulled her close and kissed the top of her head. "I'll grab some frozen pizzas from the deep freeze."

It was the stash I kept for when Avery insisted on making meals, because nine times out of ten, we ate pizza. When she first started cooking, I'd tried to force myself to eat whatever she made, but she berated me for lying, saying I needed to be honest with her—and that she'd tried her own food and knew it was terrible.

"So...what did you think about Henry?" she asked, looking up at me through her lashes.

I shook my head. "I don't like him."

She pursed her lips and raised her damn eyebrow again. "And why not?"

"He has too many tattoos," I said matter-of-factly.

Avery scoffed. "You have a lot of tattoos."

"Yeah, but I spotted one on his arm. It was a fox."

"Is there something wrong with a fox?"

"Ginny's favorite animal is a fox, Av." I sighed. "Why does this boy already have something she likes permanently tattooed on his body?"

"Do you really have any room to talk?" She pulled away and lifted my shirt.

I shivered as she traced the healed scars lining my ribs and held my breath when she kissed the little octopus. When she poked the initials she'd carved into me many years ago, she looked up at me again.

"Don't look at me like that, Av—not unless you want me to bend you over the counter and make you beg for your husband's cock."

"Tempting." She winked. "But we have company, and I'd rather not have that be the first impression we leave on the poor guy."

"Might help scare him off, though," I offered.

She shook her head and wrapped her arms around me, still looking up at me like I hung the stars. "You're not going to like anyone our baby brings home, but Ginny said she really likes him, so I need you to be nice. Trust Ginny. She wouldn't bring him around if it wasn't something special."

I didn't reply at first and found myself looking out the window to see what they were up to, praying he wasn't making any moves on my daughter in my own home.

"Rowen," Avery said sternly, demanding my attention.

"Fine, but I won't enjoy it, and if he hurts her, I'm burying his body where no one will ever find him."

"Deal." She squeezed me. "I'll even help you get rid of him if he hurts Ginny."

"That's my girl," I said before lacing my fingers through her hair, holding her in place while I kissed her.

Acknowledgements

I have to extend the first thanks to my readers as always, because without you, this duet would not have been possible. Thank you for the DMs, the letters/gifts, the constant check-ins, and the unhinged comments and conversations. You have no idea how special those moments are, and I will never forget the impact each one of you has had on my journey. To my alpha, beta, and ARC readers—WOWZA—you put up with a lot, but I can't thank you enough for helping me make Rowen and Avery's story come to life!

To El, my PA but most importantly an amazing friend, thank you for standing behind me, especially on the bad days. Thank you for putting up with my nonsense and tears, but also celebrating the victories no matter how small they were. I love you so much!!!

And to my husband, my number one fan, the love of my life. Thank you. Words aren't enough to tell you how grateful I am for your unconditional love and support, for the late nights, caffeine runs, and figuring out which positions work. You have always been my one constant, always encouraging me to do what makes me happy. I love you forever and always.

About the Author

Rhea Pryce is the pen name of a Midwest author obsessed with dark and spicy romance. She's been writing since she was little, and it was always her dream to be a published author. When she isn't busy at her most important full-time job as a stay-at-home mom or spending time with her husband and soaking up every moment she can, she's writing or reading dark, smutty books—that or distracted by social media or the latest show she's binging. Rhea refuses to stay in one box when it comes to writing, but you can always be sure whatever she releases will be dark and spicy.

You can find her on most social media apps @rheaprycewrites

www.ingramcontent.com/pod-product-compliance
Lightning Source LLC
LaVergne TN
LVHW091307150826
845673LV00006B/1562

* 9 7 9 8 9 9 1 2 8 6 3 3 6 *